SECRETS AND

An anth… the
Cambridge W… n 2023

Foreword by Sean Baker
Introduction by Harry Goode
Edited by Mary Mustard, Harry Goode & Dame Judit Hermann

Published by Cambridge Writers 2023

978-1-3999-6360-2

Cover design: Siobhán Carew © 2023

cambridgewriters.org

In memory of Steve Hammond, whose fantastic tales gave us so much pleasure.

Contents

Foreword

I had no idea what to expect when I was asked to judge this year's competition, but I have to say I enjoyed every single story and I've no doubt that any of my personal top six could have been chosen as the winner by another judge, and I wouldn't have quibbled (much!). All story competitions in the end are one person's (or sometimes a small number of people's) opinion. There was a huge variety in themes and styles, covering historic (from Ancient Greece to WW2) to several set in the future, which added to my enjoyment of the reading and judging process.

Things I was looking for that helped me come to my final decisions were: a strong start – was I engaged from the opening sentence or paragraph? Character development – did the protagonist change or develop or learn something new? Did the ending work for the story, was it satisfying? Was the dialogue appropriate for the time-period of the story and was it crisp and non-expositional? Finally, was it sufficiently clean and accurate in its grammar?

The winning six stories shared a number of structural features: small number of characters, tight timeframe and a good sense of place but, most of all, they had layers which rewarded a second and third read.

Commended:

'In The Blood' by Will Tate

I enjoyed this story for the confidence of the story-telling and the clarity of the narrative. The POV is well maintained and the three characters well drawn.

'Table Tennis' by Les Brookes

This is a sweet story, with two well-drawn main characters, and well-observed bar setting. With its tight timeframe, it packed in a lot of detail in its portrayal of two people taking their first tentative steps in a new relationship.

'63 Days in the Mind of a Smart Fridge' by Bryony Stubbs

From the title onwards, I enjoyed this a lot – such a neat, original idea with great flashes of humour and irony. The observer-narrator format suited the story and was well-handled.

Third Place:

'In Memory' By Victoria Sellar

This is a beautiful, deceptively simple story, coming in at just 1300 words. But I feel it packs a powerful emotional punch as the protagonist finds the urge to pick herself up when she visits a graveyard following the end of yet another relationship. The final image of her speaking aloud the names on the gravestones is very poignant and speaks to the change in the protagonist.

Runner-up:

'The End' by Siobhan Carew (not in this collection)

This was a tough decision – I came close to coin-toss territory with first and second. I love the voice in this story – a distinct first-person narrative about the death of someone the narrator was obsessed with. The voice has an entirely convincing naturalistic feel to it, full of repetitions and hesitations and half-formed thoughts, the vitriol the narrator felt for her arch-rival dripping off the page. And, like all three prize-winners, it had a satisfyingly ambiguous ending. It also, incidentally, sounds fantastic when read aloud with the right sort of attitude (as those present at the reading will hopefully have picked up on!).

Winner:

'In The Wash' by Emma Veit

This story works on a number of levels: on one level it's a tight piece centred on the fractious relationship between a brother and a sister set across a very short time frame as they sit in a laundrette on a stormy night. But it's also a commentary on the work of undercover police – the type of deep undercover work that has seen male officers forming long-term relationships with women, a contemporary concern that's been in the news many times in recent years. And it also works as a mystery story as the sister resorts to social media to try to find out who her brother is living with. It has superb dialogue, completely convincing in its naturalistic depiction of a sibling relationship.

And, as with the other two prize winners, it has a perfectly well-judged thought-provoking ending.

Sean Baker
April 2023

Introduction

'But there's gonna be a meter on your bed
that will disclose
what everybody knows'
Leonard Cohen, **Everybody Knows**

Immanuel Kant thought always telling the truth was a Categorical Imperative. If someone fleeing a murderer sought refuge in your house and the killer asked if you knew his potential victim's whereabouts, the moral thing was to tell him. I always think of him as a Manny No-Mates.

F Scott Fitzgerald in Tender is the Night wrote 'The strongest guard is placed on the gateway to nothing.' The ultimate secret, he suggests, being the essential emptiness of our souls.

There are overt lies and lies of omission. There are secrets concerning our lives of which we may not be consciously aware. These stories have lies and secrets of many colours and many kinds.

We are very grateful to Dr Sean Baker for acting as our judge and to Kathy English for undertaking the work of Competition Secretary. Mary Mustard has done sterling work in preparing this collection for publication and I am thankful for the assistance Judit Hermann gave me with proof reading the texts. Siobhán Carew has designed a first class cover book and performed the final work of preparation for publication.

Harry Goode
April 2023

Table Tennis

Les Brookes

- Commended -

He ought to be disappointed; the dingy brown bar, scuffed and faded, is nothing special and hardly deserves its reputation. Instead, he's relieved. What harm can come from a place that looks so ordinary?

It's taken nerve to push through the huddle of smokers at the entrance. Has anyone seen him? He dreads the thought that his parents might find out – or even worse, his college mates. Still, he's crossed the threshold and a shovel of shit has not yet dropped on his head. He's taken the first necessary step.

'Hello Jay, I'm Dev,' the message reads. 'I hope you like the selfie. I'm a British Indian studying engineering. I'd love to meet you. You have nice eyes. Do you know the Albion? I'll be there Thursday at eight.'

He glances round. Most of the tables are occupied. A couple of lone men sit on stools. No one looks like Dev. He feels awkward, hesitates, approaches the bar. The barman flaunts a frilly pink blouse, a frizz of bleached blond hair and blue teardrop earrings. 'Hi honey, first time?'

Jay grins.

'Hey, we won't bite. Now what can I get you?'

'A small Bud shandy.'

'Whoops! Don't go mad.'

The barman smiles, delivers the drink, pats him on the cheek. Jay moves to a vacant table and sits watching the scene.

After a while he glances at his watch. Ten past eight. He still feels acutely uncomfortable, as if all eyes are fixed on him. Shortly, a man approaches and sits at his table. A tattooed heavyweight in a black string vest and bulging jeans.

'Mind if I join you?'

'Ah well ... I'm waiting for someone, actually.'

'Really? That's funny, so am I ... Anyone, actually ...You look nice.'

Jay smiles and looks away. The man gets up. 'Hey, relax, kid, no pressure.' He raises a thumb and saunters to the bar. Jay pulls out his phone and pretends to read. Suddenly a young woman appears. 'Hello, I'm Anita.' He looks up, startled. 'Sorry to bother you.' He smiles. 'Anyway, my friend Adam' – she points to a pale youth across the room – 'would really like to meet you, but he's terribly shy. Would you like to join us?'

Jay glances across the room. Adam waves timidly and gives a weak smile. 'Oh ... I'm sorry ... You see, I'm waiting for someone.'

'Ah, shame. He'll be so disappointed. He deserves a break. He never gets off with anyone.' She smiles and drifts back to Adam, who waves again ... sadly.

Jay returns to his phone, surfs for news and scans several sites, including one entitled 'How to Manage a Blind Date'.

Twenty minutes later he again looks at his watch. Eight-thirty. He's been stood up. He struggles with hurt and disappointment. He drains his glass in a single gulp, jumps to his feet and makes for the door. But just as he gets there, someone comes bursting through. 'Jay? ... Are you Jay?'

He nods blankly.

'Message from Dev. He'll be here soon. Please don't go.'

He stares in confusion.

'I'm Jamila, by the way ... Sorry, can't stop – I'm late for my dance class.' She smiles, plants a kiss on his cheek and exits.

He returns to his seat and stares at his empty glass. What now? Same again, or something special? ... Can he afford a cocktail? A Brandy Alexander, say, or a Screwdriver? ... Or even something saucy? A French Kiss? A Pornstar? Sex on the Beach?

He looks up. A tall man with a mop of green hair, his pale white legs extending from baggy leather shorts, has just entered. He and the barman whisper together and burst into shrieks of neighing laughter.

Jay returns to his phone. 'Dev,' he writes, 'where are you? Please rescue me. I'm desperate.' He tosses the phone onto the table and almost instantly it buzzes. He snatches it up and is dismayed to see that it's Richie. He thinks about not answering, then snaps on. 'Richie, I can't hang about – I'm in the middle of something.'

'You're in the middle of something? What about me? Someone stole my bag at the gym. Yeah, my bag. I'm not making this up. With my wallet, my cards, my equipment and twenty something bloody quid. Yeah, and what's more I've got a suspicion who it is. There's this creep who hangs around the lockers ...'

Jay keeps the phone to his ear but stops listening. Richie continues without missing a beat until Jay breaks in. 'Richie, I'm really sorry about your bag, but I repeat, I'm in the middle of something.'

'Middle of something? Middle of what?'

'I'll explain later ... A kind of rendezvous.'

'Wow, you sly dog. Who is she?'

'Richie, will you please get the fuck off.'

'Oh thanks.' Richie's rattle continues until he's cut dead.

Jay closes his eyes in search of composure and, when he opens them, a figure is striding towards him. A smiling figure in jeans and a white T-shirt, whose lean dark face is crowned with sleek black hair. Jay knows the face well; it's not the first time it's held his gaze. 'Jay?'

'Dev.'

'Jay, I'm so sorry.'

'It's okay ... Getting a bit desperate, though ... Sent a message.'

'Ah, missed it ... Probably locking my bike.'

Dev sits. They smile and gaze at each other. There's an awkward pause and they shift, wondering how to begin.

Jay kicks off. 'Pardon the cliché,' he grins, 'but do you come here often?'

'Not often,' says Dev. 'I dodge in when no one's looking. How about you?' 'First time. I slid in like an undercover agent, wondering who I'd meet. What if I ran into Nobby Clark, my P.E. teacher?'

'Ah, no problem – he'd be more alarmed than you.'

They splutter, giggle, crack up. It's a breakthrough, a bonding. Jay begins to relax and Dev points to the empty glass.

'Anyway, what can I get you?'

'Actually' – Jay pauses, afraid to sound extravagant – 'I was thinking about ... a cocktail.'

'Oh wild! ... Something saucy? ... A One-Night-Stand? ... An Orgasm?' Jay blushes.

'Hey, steady on ... Perhaps a Brandy Alexander? ... I'll pay.'

Dev grins. 'Thinking about my bank balance, you may have to.'

He gets up, moves to the bar and returns with two long-stemmed glasses filled with thick brown cream topped with nutmeg. They sit back, sipping luxuriously.

'Mmm, good one,' moans Dev. 'Anyway, I take it you saw Jamila?'

'Yes,' says Jay – then hesitates, wary of sounding pushy: 'So who is she?'

Dev shifts. 'She's ... well ...' He twirls his glass. 'Let's call her my girlfriend.'

'Your girlfriend?'

Dev shrugs. 'Well ... you know ... just for my parents.'

Jay frowns. 'You mean ... she's your cover?'

'If you like.'

'Does she know?'

'Of course – she's perfectly happy with it.'

Jay sips his cocktail. He's dated a couple of girls. He and Amber were pushed together by his mates, and later Kerry attached herself to him at a party. Neither girl lasted long, and he felt nothing but relief when they broke up. He hated the fondling, the petting, the sly fingers caressing his lips. But the experience had one clear benefit: it taught him who he was, what he wanted.

'Do you have to pretend, Dev?'

'Yes. My parents are strictly traditional. They'd turn me out or force me into marriage with a woman.'

'Times have changed, Dev.'

'Not my parents.' Dev looks away, then turns back with a shrug. 'Still ... we can at least be honest with each other.' He lifts an eyebrow. 'Your name, for instance – is that a cover?'

'Jay for Jordan,' grins Jay.

'Hm, nice – but I prefer Jay.'

Jay chuckles. 'And Dev?'

'Actually Vik – for Vikram.'

'Hm, nice – but I prefer Dev.'

'Okay, let's stick with Jay and Dev.'

They laugh, and Jay studies the face before him. A keen, boyish face with sharp eyes. Eyes that fix him with a hard gleam mixed with latent softness. He lowers his gaze. Jay and Dev, he muses. A cosy pairing, but can it last? Dev is afraid of being turned out, and what about himself? Does he have the courage to confront his parents, not to mention the taunts at college? He's heard the names flung out without provocation: pouf, queer, bender. How much worse if you were to lay claim to them, flaunt your queerness.

'It's good to see you,' he says. 'I thought I'd been stood up.'

'Sorry. I work till late, then get home and fall asleep.'

Jay settles back. 'So, tell me about yourself.'

'What d'you want to know? I have an older sister and a younger brother. Dad drives a van, Mum works at a checkout. We all fight like hell.' Dev grins and spreads his palms. 'And you?'

'My parents are teachers. They sit marking all night. I have a sister, Josie, who fortunately likes boys – something we share – so I'm hoping she'll provide the grandchildren.'

They chuckle and talk some more. They touch on Hinduism, books, music, travel, food, films, men who chat online.

'My go,' says Jay. 'Same again?'

'Ah no,' says Dev. 'But it's a lovely night out there. Fancy a walk?'

Jay smiles and nods; and as they leave, he sees that Adam is chatting to the man in the string vest. He catches Anita's eye, and they grin. Has the lad finally struck gold? It's almost midsummer. Outside, it's balmy and still, the sky lit by a faint afterglow, the streets noisy with whooping teenagers. Dev unlocks his bike. They stroll through the market square, strewn with litter from the locked-up stalls, then turn down Chapel Street to the river. There's scarcely a soul on the towpath. Dev parks his bike, and they sit on a bench watching a cluster of swans on the bank. Dev reaches for Jay's hand and Jay tenses with an electric thrill. They smile at each other, then gaze ahead. A small, flop-eared dog arrives and snuffles round their feet. A man passes, mumbles a greeting and calls the dog to heel.

After a while they uncouple and move on. They say nothing, but as they pass under the George Bridge, Dev steers Jay into shadow. He pulls him close, stroking his neck, fanning his cheeks with warm breath, crushing his mouth to his lips. Jay yields in a daze, then responds instinctively, his heart fluttering. A surge floods his face and his head reels. He's never kissed a boy before. He presses closer, swooning to the sensation, then pulls away. It's too much. In any case, he's spotted a couple approaching. He nods to Dev, who glances over his shoulder, and they break apart.

They wander on past the mill, then turn back into town.

'We could try the park,' says Dev. 'It's pretty quiet at night.'

'I need to get home, Dev. My parents will worry. They think I'm playing table tennis. I'm usually in by ten.'

'Table tennis,' breathes Dev. 'Wow.'

They eye each other, splutter, giggle, crack up.

'Okay, but may I walk you home, as they say in the old movies?'

Jay hesitates. Is this a good idea? What if they're seen? What if word gets back to his parents and they ask questions? Is it wise to show Dev where he lives, to drop his guard after just one night? He scans the face before him. Can he trust Dev? Well, of course he can. He chides himself. Dev is lovely – kind, sensitive, an open book. It's written all over him, shines out of his eyes.

'Okay,' he nods, 'I'd like that.'

'In that case, lead on.'

They trail through the streets to the tick of Dev's back wheel, stopping to watch a chef grill steak in a restaurant and the daredevil antics of skateboarders in a playground. Then, in Telford Place, Jay, seized with sudden panic, brings them to a halt.

'This is it,' he says. 'Where I live.'

'This big old place?' says Dev. 'Telford Lodge?'

Jay nods, and Dev whistles. 'Hey, what a swank! I didn't take you for a rich kid.' Jay blushes, and glances round. There's no one in the street. He leans forward, kisses Dev on the mouth. 'Can we meet again next Thursday? Same time, same place?'

'That's a whole week,' grins Dev.

'We can stay in touch. Don't call me, though – just keep texting.'

'Okay, prepare for a blitz.'

Dev strokes Jay's cheek, mounts his bike, waves, rounds the corner.

Jay waits, then walks briskly in the other direction. He turns into Osborne Terrace, reaches for his key and enters the door of Number 8.

His parents are marking at the kitchen table. They barely look up.

'So how was it?' his mum asks.

'Okay,' he replies.

'Okay?' she mutters. 'Is that all?'

'Well ... you know ... lively.'

'Jesus,' his dad growls. 'Cryptic as ever.'

He drifts into the sitting room and flops onto the sofa. It's been a great night, a thrilling breakthrough. He's still high, still excited, still floating. His only regret is his loss of nerve. What possessed him to say he lived at the Lodge? And what right had he to taunt Dev about Jamila? Should he text him now and confess?

His phone buzzes. 'Great night,' he reads. 'Can't wait to see you again.'

'Nor me,' he replies, then plunges: 'Dev, I'm sorry. I don't live in that house. I was just covering myself.'

He waits anxiously.

'Thought so – or teachers' salaries have risen.'

'Dev, how do we end this pretence?'

'Dunno. Be brave. We'll find a way.'

Jay frowns. How to respond? Dev jumps in. 'Jay, can we discuss this some other time? I have a long day tomorrow.'

'Okay, but keep texting. Don't go dead on me.'

'Go dead on you? I'm your greatest fan.'

Jay giggles. 'You giddy romantic.'

'Giddy yourself.'

Then, after a pause: 'Jay, I must go. Enough table tennis.'

A love heart follows.

Jay smiles. 'Great match, though.'

He returns the heart, snaps off, sits musing.

Find a way? What way? All ways seem disastrous. He snaps on again and turns up a website entitled 'How to Come Out'. Don't feel forced, it says. Be gradual. Choose someone you trust, a close friend or family member.

Hm, all very well, but what about Dev? Can you be Hindu and gay? He turns up another site. Attitudes vary, he reads. The scriptures neither condemn nor condone. The Kamasutra affirms and recognises same-sex relations. The sculptures in some Hindu temples depict scenes of orgiastic pansexual abandon. Wow!

He settles back, shuts his eyes, decides to tackle one day at a time. He's taken a big step tonight. They'll meet again next week. He feels strong, proud, elated. Be brave. They can beat this. *Just do it*, as the T-shirts proclaim.

Island Games

Beth Cooke

It is dark when I step off the bus; not the same dark as the one under which I left the island, that was an excited, silent dark that seismically shifted in a split second, twice. This dark is full of music and chatter drifting over the balmy air from the fast-food restaurant on the other side of the street where tourists, and the odd local, enjoy their evenings with burgers and fries. I have been in the country long enough to know how to find the cheaper, local food, and walk away.

Even before the bell tinkles, I feel their eyes on me. They noticed me through the window, communicated their concern with sideways glances so that the whole family turn to watch as I enter. I step over the threshold of the small shop. I pick up a bag of Amplang, the fish crackers I tried as a dare when I first arrived that turned out to be a surprisingly tasty snack. The familiar boxes of Chips Ahoy catch my eye, and I can almost taste the cookies inside, but I know I must make my funds last. Suspicious eyes follow me as I take my meagre purchase to the till, trying not to reveal my anxiety over how little cash I had left.

It had not been this way when I arrived in the capital two months previously. We had been a big group then, with bright eyes wide with wonder at the world we had entered. In the big city we were welcomed with friendly smiles wherever we went. I had met the others only once before boarding the plane, at a training weekend in Kent. I took the train from Cambridge on a bright, early spring morning to meet the marine research team I was to spend three months in the field with. By the time we travelled to Borneo, I had finished my first year at university. The long summer stretching before me promised to be filled with underwater adventures on the other side of the world. I sat next to Tim on the plane, the tall, blonde lead researcher on the expedition. I had felt a little shy at first, choosing to read my book, risking a sideways glance at him every few minutes, intimidated by his laid-back surfer look and his intellect. He caught one of my glances and a smile lit up the corner of his mouth.

'You're reading the Haunting of Hill House?' he said, 'Great book. I went to a haunted house once, didn't see any actual ghosts mind, but weird stuff happened. You know, doors slamming, light bulbs flickering, the works. Creepy. Ah, dinner, I love plane food. Don't you?'

By the time we stepped out into the tropical warmth of Kota Kinabalu, we had become friends.

For a few weeks we studied coral and fish identification in the clean, air-conditioned classrooms at the University of Malaysia, before returning to the hot, dusty city centre to sit on white plastic garden chairs in small, noisy cafes and enjoy nasi goreng washed down with a beer. While we studied, Tim kept busy gathering bundles of food, roll mats, mosquito nets; stacked them in the corridors of the youth hostel ready to be strapped to the top of the minibus that would take us north.

On our final night in KK, we wandered through the shiny air-conditioned shopping centre for a last taste of civilisation, before heading to the fish market. Squeezed in between market stalls were yet more plastic chairs where we perched to enjoy the last meal that we would not have to cook for ourselves. I sat next to Tim, chatted and joked, balmy sea air wafted around us, bringing with it the scent of raw and cooked fish. I went to bed happy, in a dorm room of new friends excited for the next day's journey.

I was woken by Tim's alarm clock blaring, a familiar sound by now. I had always been one to get up at the very last minute I could get away with, but not Tim. He enjoyed a leisurely morning routine and seemed to take pleasure in making everyone else get up too early too. Once the sleep cleared from my brain enough to remember what day it was, for the first time I had been keen to get up too. Our final hostel breakfast of soft toast, washed down with black tea, was hastily consumed before we loaded up the minibus and set off. Four hours later we were boarding a ferry in Kudat that would take us to Banggi Island where our expedition leaders, Gregg and Simon, were waiting with the small dive boat that would need to make several trips to get us, our kit, and the supplies, across the water to a smaller, otherwise uninhabited island that was to be our home for the next eight weeks.

'Welcome to Pulau Balak!' Gregg said as he anchored the boat just offshore.

We jumped down into the clear warm water and waded the last few meters to the beach. Our house was on stilts at one end of the beach, the 'self-flushing' toilet nestled in the mangroves at the other. Once we unrolled our sleeping mats and hung up our mosquito nets, we gathered round the large table to finalise our plans.

'So, as you know we will be diving six days a week' Simon had started in his business-like manner. 'We've split you into three groups for chores and you'll rotate through them - see the board over there. Whoever is on breakfast duty, make sure you're awake enough that you don't use sea water to make the porridge. Yes, that has happened before! Oh, and by the way, that is Porridge, the cat, he's incredibly ugly and probably too old to catch any rats now, but he's friendly enough. Any questions?'

The next few weeks had been an excited blur. Gradually we all passed our SCUBA training, and fish identification tests, learned how to do underwater surveys and analyse the data.

Now he was back with the other leaders, Tim withdrew and spent his time with them rather than mixing with us volunteers. I often spotted him huddled with Simon in the evenings, whist Gregg did the data entry on the computer, a slow job as the machine was often inhabited by ants. Our easy friendship from the plane had evaporated.

As Sunday was our only dive free day, Saturday night was party night. We carefully rationed the vodka to make sure it would last the expedition, but between us we had brought enough to have a good time. It was on a Saturday night that Tim suggested the game. Something to keep us entertained now that we had all passed our tests and didn't need to spend so much time studying. A murder mystery.

He carefully wrote everyone's name on a piece of paper and handed each of us two more.

'Now I need each of you to write a place on the island on one, and some sort of 'murder weapon' on the other,' he instructed. 'We'll mix them up before each of you picks one from each pot.'

The premise was simple. 'Kill' your victim before someone 'killed' you. I picked out Mary, the quiet blond girl who had received most of the attention walking through the streets of KK, yet received the least now we were away from the locals.

A fun idea at the start, it wasn't long before the game made everyone a little paranoid. Not wanting to be the first to succumb, I kept a close eye on everyone whilst we cleaned the house the following day. I would have to wait until Monday morning when we were next out diving to tap Mary on the shoulder with my regulator hose in the dive store and say 'Gotcha'. It should be easy, if I 'lived' that long.

Luckily, with another four weeks to go, everyone seemed to be playing the long game, and an unsuspecting Mary was the first to be claimed by the game the next morning. I felt bad doing it, but relieved not to be the first myself. Once the shocked look eased from her face, she passed the details of her victim on to me.

I spent days wondering how I was going to lure Gregg to the generator shed and bop him with a frying pan. This had preoccupied me so much that I almost forgot to watch my own back. Yet somehow, I survived whilst others around me had fallen and passed on their slips of paper to the next person. By the time the next Saturday night party rolled round, half of the group were out of the game. Tim began quizzing everyone, finding it acceptable to speak to us volunteers now, as he tried to find out who other people had. The following morning, Tim and I found ourselves alone after breakfast, each nursing a sore head. He slid along the bench closer to me.

'Not many of us left now, eh?' he said. Perhaps this was it, I thought. Perhaps Tim's papers said 'Becca', 'dining room bench', 'a spoon'.

'Not many? Oh, you mean in the game. Nope, it's getting closer now.' He picked up a spoon, leant a little closer, I held my breath.

He sat back, stirred sugar into his black tea, took a sip. When he had put the spoon back down on the table I exhaled. I realised what he wanted before he opened his mouth again.

'Who'd you get then? Need any help?'

There it was, predictable, but useful. I had still not managed to come up with any way of getting Gregg to the genny shed without him seeing me or guessing what was going on. Remembering the plane, I decided I could trust Tim, I glanced around to make sure no one was listening and whispered my mission.

'Ha!' he guffawed, 'good one! How’re you gonna to do that?'

'I’ve been wondering that for days, there’s no way.'

'That’s where you’re wrong, Becca.' The shock that he had remembered my name after weeks of ignoring me had not stopped me leaning in to hear his plan.

We dived the Misplaced Reef the next morning; loaded the boat early and headed out to conduct our surveys. It was so peaceful below the water, flat calm above. When we returned to camp, I wandered back up the beach chatting to the others, ready to begin cooking a dinner of curry served with the roti we’d found a recipe for in the handwritten camp cookbook.

After dinner, whilst the others were feeling full and sleepy, I slipped from the house and found the frying pan I had stashed next to the oil drum oven earlier. Tim had shown me how to switch off the generator. 'Gregg will have to come if the power goes out', he explained.

As I rounded the corner of the shed, I switched on my head torch. With a final glance around I reached out a hand and flipped the switch. The engine sputtered out and the house was plunged into darkness. I hid behind a tree, my thumping heart threatening to give me away. I heard distant commotion from the house and then, closer, the voices of Gregg and Simon approaching the shed, looking in to see what was wrong. Slowly I took a step closer, then two, then three. I was right behind them, one hand reached out to tap Gregg on the shoulder, the other clutched the frying pan.

Gregg jumped and turned to look at me, his concerned look turned first to confusion then annoyance when he saw the frying pan. 'What? Who's that? This isn't the time...' he started, as Simon flicked the switch. The genny roared to life.

Simon turned the torch, lit up Gregg's face. A shot rang out amongst the palm trees. Gregg looked at me in shocked disbelief, then fell forwards.

'Shit! Gregg! Gregg! Jeeze, get help! Somebody get help!' Simon, shouting, confused, leaning over Gregg, shaking him by the shoulders. I backed away. I had lured Gregg up there. Whatever had just happened, I had played a part in it. Shit, I had been set up! He had set me up! Tim had handed out the names, could easily have manipulated the whole thing.

Simon's shouting had brought the others from the house, crashing through the undergrowth in their haste to see what had happened. Now was my chance. I ran back to the dorm room, through the door, slammed into something, which turned out to be somebody. Expecting to see the uniform of one of the armed Malay police who had stayed with us at the beginning of the expedition, I slowly raised my eyes taking in the dusty sandals, khaki shorts and blue t-shirt Tim had been wearing. Fear turning to horror as my gaze reached his face, saw his corner of the mouth smile, felt his hands cup my face then his lips on my forehead.

'Gotcha Becca!' he murmured. 'In the dorm room, with a kiss.'

'But, wait. What? Gregg?' I stammered.

'Yeah, sorry about that.' He blushed. 'Didn't realise the

guys were such good actors, or how loud the firecracker would sound with the genny off. It's just I've been wanting to do this since the plane and with everyone always around I, well I needed a distraction.'

For the first time, I noticed his hands still held me, and he bent closer again, asked 'Is it OK if I kiss you again, but here?' brushed my lips with the tips of his thumbs.

In most stories, my knees would have given way whilst any remaining hint of fury at Tim's actions melted away. But this is real-life sugar. I cannot deny my knees wobbled a little, but I was fuming, had been ready to flee in a boat I didn't know how to drive, across a sea I couldn't navigate, in the dark, on my own. Sorry Timothy, but you went too far.

Now, here I am, halfway across the country having abandoned the expedition and convinced a very sheepish Gregg to drop me at Kudat, about to pay for my snacks surrounded by an air of suspicion.

'*Terima kasih*.' Handing over my Ringgit I offered my thanks in Malay. In an instant the suspicion turned to smiles. As I was waved from the shop as an equal, I was sure of two things. I had no regrets about ditching the project, or the scheming, albeit handsome, Tim. And I was not going back to KK, at least not just yet. My flight home was not for another couple of weeks. Across road my eye caught a poster advertising expedition to the summit of Mount Kinabalu, the office would still be open if I hurried. I would start an adventure, and always be honest, and always an equal.

Fish cracker anyone?

Would You Believe It?

Helen Culnane

The landlord gawped at the sheet of paper being held up by a man who had just purchased a pint of bitter. 'Well, would you believe that?'

'I got it off the web,' said the stranger. 'There's no photo but I thought it sounded interesting so I printed it off thinking I would come and take a look for myself.'

He read aloud. 'For Sale. Tanglewood Croft, Tanglewood Lane, Westonby. A three-bedroom cottage, lounge, kitchen and bathroom. Ripe for Restoration'

'I found Westonby, easy enough on my sat-nav, but I've driven round and round this village, I can't for the life of me locate Tanglewood Lane.'

'That's hardly surprising,' replied the landlord. 'It's no better than a footpath these days; more tangle than lane, if you get my meaning. You'd certainly not get a car anywhere near.'

'If there's a footpath, though, I could walk there. After driving all the way out here from Manchester, the least I can do is to take a look at the property, see if it's got potential.'

The landlord addressed his regulars congregated at the far end of the bar, 'Got a fellow here wants to look at the house down Tanglewood Lane.'

An old man, perched on a high stool confirmed, 'There is a house down there, right enough.'

One of the lads loitering around the snooker table sauntered over to inform him, 'It's a witch's house, that is.'

'You should hear the howling when the moon is full,' quipped one of his mates. 'Waaaaahhhhh....'

The stranger shook his head at the youths.

Another lad chipped in. 'My dad says she lays traps to catch kids that go too near.'

'Your Dad's famous for his tall tales,' remarked the landlord.

'No, he's not.'

'Well how come she never grabbed him, then? He was forever scrumping her apples.'

Another regular commented, 'Your dad's so fat and greasy she probably didn't fancy him.'

Ignoring the insult, the lad draped a conspiratorial arm around the stranger's shoulder and confided, 'Ignore this lot, mate; they don't know what they're talking about. It's wolves that does the howling in the wood, not witches.'

'That's right. Witches moan,' said his pal.

'Nah, the moaning's ghosts. You should hear them on Halloween when they come out to look for human blood.'

The smallest child in a family party eating Sunday lunch at the table by the window screwed up her face and wailed, 'Are ghosts going eat our blood?'

'Oh, don't listen in on other people's conversations,' scolded her mother. 'That way, all you ever hear is lies. There's no ghosts in the Tanglewood, and no witches, nor wolves, nor haunted houses neither. Now, eat up your vegetables or there will be no ice cream for afters.'

The stranger picked up his pint and moved along the bar

to sit on the stool next to the old man's. 'Lived in the village long?' he enquired.

'Eighty-four years, man and boy.'

'That's a fair old innings. It must be the good country air that keeps you going.'

'Aye son,' he raised an empty glass and mused, 'that and the good country ale.'

Chuckling at the presumption of the man, the stranger hailed the landlord and ordered 'A pint for my friend here, if you please.'

His glass refilled, the man tilted it towards his benefactor who then enquired, 'So, apart from good air and good ale, what else does this village have to offer a townie on the lookout for a place in the country? Other than haunted houses in the woods, that is?'

A man in a cloth cap nodded. 'That'd be Bart's place.'

'Bart?' The stranger raised a quizzical eyebrow.'

Replies came thick and fast. 'Bart the fart.' 'Village idiot' 'Stinky tramp.'

'Oooh, that is not fair,' protested a woman sipping sherry with her cronies around a low table in the ingle nook. 'Bart was never the sharpest pin in the packet, but a kinder, gentler soul you could never meet. That house may be falling down, but it is his house; so, if it suits him who are you to criticize?'

'You say house; I'd call it a shack.'

'It wasn't always like that,' put in the waitress carrying plates piled high with roast dinner towards the dining area. 'When I was a girl that was the prettiest place. It had a painted veranda all along one side with deck chairs on it, and flowerpots and there was a strawberry patch and an orchard. A proper fairy place, it was.'

'Ah,' remarked one of the sherry drinkers, 'that would have been in Bart's auntie's time.'

'Mrs Caldwell?' scoffed a man in a cloth cap. 'She were no fairy, that one.'

His mates agreed 'If ever there was a witch, it was Minnie Caldwell.'

'You watch who you're calling names,' countered the sharp-tongued sherry drinker. 'Mrs Caldwell was a fine lady; Chair of the WI, Chair of the Parish Council too.'

'Huh, chair of bloody everything that one,' he retorted.

'Indeed she was, and whatever job she took on she always did it proud. They don't make them like that anymore, folks who'll work for any good cause, be it in the village or up in town or ....'

'Anywhere in the world; didn't she volunteer at the Oxfam shop?'

The man on the stool muttered, 'Her and collecting boxes.' Those who did remember instinctively clamped hands over pockets.

'Well, the woman obviously had more money than she knew what to do with,' remarked a fellow in muddy dungarees. 'The clothes she used to wear; all dressed up like she lady muck on her way to take tea with the Queen, not a do-gooder going to work in a charity shop.'

'You know, I reckon that's where she got all that fancy

stuff from, the Oxfam shop?'

'They were hand-me-downs from posh houses?'

While regulars continued to deride Mrs Caldwell's wardrobe, one of the sherry drinkers announced, 'Of course, she wasn't really Bart's aunt, you know.'

'No, not proper family,' chirped her friend.

'She took the lad in after her daughter went off to university,' confirmed another.

'Ah,' a retired teacher from the grammar school heaved a sigh and announced to nobody in particular. 'Evangeline Caldwell - a clever girl, very clever. Went on to Oxford, you know? Got a double first.'

'Believe that if you will,' muttered a woman.

'It's not the story I heard,' agreed her friend.

'What did you hear?'

'Her Ma packed her off somewhere with a bun in the oven.'

'Never!'

'Well, she was asking for it, wasn't she, the way she flounced about the place.'

'She may have been asking for it,' muttered a man, 'but she never delivered on the promise.'

'Right prick teaser, she was. All the lads fancied her, but she was never slow to let us know she was too good for the likes of us.'

'But you have to admit, she was easily the prettiest girl in the village. She got chosen as Gala Queen three years in succession.'

'She did that. You'd expect a girl who'd won the contest once, would stand aside to give someone else have a chance the next year.'

'Well, let's be honest, none of the rest of us could have looked half as good as she did in the robe and crown, riding at the head of the parade on that chestnut pony she had.'

'Oh, she had it all, that one; brains, beauty and a horse of her own.'

Eyeing the school master, a woman asked 'D'you reckon Chalky was soft on her? What was it he said? 'Clever, very clever'.' Her companions suppressed giggles, as did the men at the bar, while mulling over their versions of the tale.

'Like mother, like daughter,' said one. 'She might have been a looker, but she'd have been hell to live with.'

'If my daughter flaunted herself the way that one did, I'd take my belt to her, so help me, I would.'

'But Evangeline Caldwell didn't have a father to keep her on the straight and narrow, did she?'

'No, no she didn't; just that dragon of a mother.'

'Where was her father then?'

'Wasn't he killed in a car crash somewhere?' asked the cloth cap man. 'Well, that's the story his missus put out.'

'Once she got over her tears.'

'Oh remember that, the way she cried and cried.'

'Ah but what if he didn't die? What if he just walked out on her? I mean, how could a man retain his self-respect, married to a bossy cow like her?'

'Do you think they were ever married in the first place?' mused the man on the bar stool. 'Nobody here had ever seen or heard of them until they turned up in the village, complete with motor car, washing machine, fridge and a new-born babe.'

'The baby was christened in the village church.'

'She was, but there never was a funeral for the husband. You'd think with the mother being so devout ....'

Silence descended on the pub as the clientele considered this proposition.

'I remember her funeral, though,' mused the landlord. 'What a wake that was; everyone in the village came, not to mention the great and the good from all around. Maisie and me had to take on extra staff to help with the catering.'

'Who booked the pub for that?'

'Wasn't it the Vicar?'

'Probably, he was like that. And you couldn't expect Bart to organise something like that, could you?'

'A ha'penny off the shilling, was Bart.'

'Bart was a charity case,' the waitress explained in response to questions from a group of diners from the new estate. 'Mrs Caldwell took him in from some home for hard-to-place orphans.'

'What a kind thing to do.'

The waitress shrugged. 'Kind is as kind does. The woman was probably lonely with her husband dead and her daughter left home.'

The diners nodded. 'Empty nest syndrome.'

'Either that or she couldn't live without somebody to boss around. But give her fair dues, she gave that lad a good home and anyone could see that he worshipped her.'

'It is odd, when you think about it, though,' mused a sherry drinker. 'I mean, when the woman had a daughter of her own, you'd think she'd leave the house to her, not a man so soft in the head he could hardly look after himself, never mind maintain the property.'

'Do you reckon that was why Evangeline didn't come to her mother's funeral?'

'I don't think that girl showed her face in the village once after she left. An ungrateful child like that doesn't deserve an inheritance.'

'I suppose not, but to leave it to a simpleton...'

'It was Bart's home. He'd never have settled any place else.'

The stranger asked, 'So why do you think Bart's put it on the market now?'

'Oh no, it's not Bart who's selling.'

'Can't be. He died six months ago.'

'Terrible thing that was,' commented the man in dungarees. 'Mrs Miller at the shop was worried. He'd not been in buying cakes and biscuits for a while – and that was not like him; he did love his cakes and biscuits. So, a bunch of us took it on ourselves to go into the woods to investigate. We found him on his kitchen floor. He'd been there for weeks to judge by the smell. And the flies...'

'Hey, enough of that!' The landlord interrupted, nodding in the direction of the dining tables. 'There's people come here to enjoy their lunch; they don't want gruesome stories served up with their best English lamb.'

'Whatever,' said a woman 'Evangeline never did come back to claim the place, did she?'

'I dare say she'll have bagged herself some smart country gent with a large estate by now,' remarked a woman. 'What would someone like that want with a tumbledown shack in a field at the end of an impenetrable lane that leads to nowhere.'

'That's how you'd describe this Tanglewood Croft, is it?' asked the stranger.

The woman nodded and a man backed her up. 'That's precisely what anyone fool enough to buy that place will find he's landed himself with.'

'So, it needs a lot doing to it?'

Everyone agreed that that would be putting it mildly. The only thing to do with a place like Bart's was to pull it down and start again from scratch.

The landlord asked the stranger, 'That's not why you're here is it, to buy somewhere cheap so you can do it up and sell it on for a fortune?'

'You're not with one of those TV make-over shows, are you?' asked one man while another sneered, 'You'll be on a high jump to nothing if you think you could do a restoration job on that place.'

The stranger assured them, 'Oh no, no. No, I'm not thinking of that.' Which was a lie.

Restore that cottage as a surprise for his mother's fiftieth birthday was the first thing he had thought of when he received the solicitor's letter informing him of his unexpected inheritance. However, having listened to the locals talk, he had to agree with his father who had had vetoed his plan and insisted he say not a word to his mother.

There were aspects of Eva's childhood home, her husband said, that had been idyllic; the hills and the woods and the pony that inspired her life-long love of horses, but Westonby had other, darker, associations. There had been a rape, he confided, banishment to the city and the abandonment of her baby to the care of nuns who ran the maternity home for single mothers. That time had left a permanent scar on his mother's heart. She hid it well, but it was still there, despite her years at university, her career, her marriage to him and the birth of their son. It would do nobody any favours to open up that old wound.

Having listened to the locals, the stranger had to conclude that his father had been right. The only thing he could do with his inheritance, was to contact the solicitor and the estate agent and tell them to go ahead and advertise the property for sale.

Bianca Lavet and The End of All Things

Mike English

Hello, and welcome to my vlog: The End of All Things. My name's Bianca Lavet; you probably know me best as the only person to have won 'Investigative Journalist Of The Year' three years running. That was for 2026, 2027 and 2028 as it happens. Later, I shall fill you in as to what I have been doing after the BBC dropped me like a hot potato, as soon after Cumbriagate as they decently could, but first let me fill you in as to what really happened at Cumbriagate. As you probably remember, the IPCC COP 31 in 2026 appeared to be a watershed moment in the fight against climate change. To the annoyance of certain Arab countries who resigned from the IPCC in protest, the world agreed not only to phase out fossil fuel, but to end its use altogether. Most countries criminalized the production and use of coal, oil and natural gas. Some, perhaps, went too far. Russia mandated the death penalty for using fossil fuel and even televised a few executions, which, although not broadcast by the BBC, did get Al Jazeera its best ever ratings.

In December 2026, I received an email from Ken Strike, a geologist who claimed to be a local convener for Extinction Rebellion. He had issues with a new copper mine near Whitehaven, which was due to open in a few weeks. Apparently, the sources of copper ore in Cumbria were confined to Skiddaw slates or volcanic areas of hard rhyolite. Ken turned about to be as bearded as he sounded. As far as he was concerned there was no copper anywhere near Whitehaven, so what was going on? I had no idea what Skiddaw slates were, but I could smell a story, so I showed the email and my meeting notes to my editor, who pulled a few strings and shortly I had a job as a trainee chef with West Cumbria Mining.

Some of the other new starters complained about southerners taking jobs that had been promised to locals, but they weren't a bad sort really, just beaten down by life. I could cope with a little prejudice. At least no one spotted my hidden camera and microphone.

I hit pay dirt that first lunch time. One of the miners came in coughing and wheezing. He started complaining loudly about coal dust and the cough that had killed his grandfather.

Within moments he was set upon by security and led away. Everyone seemed to know who he was, so it wasn't difficult to track him down at his local pub later that evening. After a few drinks he was still remarkably uncommunicative. I guessed he had signed some sort of gagging clause to ensure a decent pay off. When I mentioned that I worked for the BBC, he suggested rather gruffly, that I look in the hoppers where the copper ore was stored before being shipped to the smelter. The next day I managed to get a peek. Unexpectedly the ore was a shiny black. I broke off a piece, and that evening did the famous monologue to camera where I smeared my face with 'copper ore' that looked for all the world just like coal.

So that was Cumbriagate. There were a great many casualties high up in the BBC, apparently our journalism had been unbalanced, and I myself was let go a mere three months later.

A few years afterwards at COP 36, the IPCC acknowledged that despite the world reaching net zero in

2027, the IPCC had failed, the average world temperature had exceeded 1.5C above 1850 levels in every month of the previous year. It also emerged that to prevent world average temperatures exceeding 2C above 1850 levels it would be necessary to prevent atmospheric greenhouse gas concentrations reaching 445 parts per million carbon dioxide equivalent. The Mauna Loa greenhouse gas concentrations for October were published on the closing day of the COP showing 446 ppm carbon dioxide. Fortunately, it would take decades for the world temperature to rise, so the human race had perhaps, forty years to bring the carbon dioxide level down and stop temperatures actually reaching 2 degrees above 1850 values. You may remember my rather emotional vlog for this day, where I ranted about why this couldn't have been done earlier. Nobody seemed to have an answer, merely repeating the platitude that nobody had known what was going on. Within an hour of uploading my vlog I had an email from one of the refugee camps on the outskirts of Bishop's Stortford. It was the same Ken Strike, who had put me onto the Cumbian 'copper' mine. He remembered a meeting of the Cambridge University of The Third Age Environment Group where a speaker had presented the facts that the IPCC had clearly ignored. He even had an address for the speaker.

Unfortunately, the address was slap bang in the middle of the Cambridge Hot Zone. For those of you who have been sleeping for the last decade I should explain that when Vladimir Putin executed his retributive strike at the end of the Ukraine War in 2024. Only three of his nuclear missiles actually exploded, and only one was a thermonuclear detonation, the one targeting Cambridge. That said fission bombs do a lot of damage as the people of Lyons and Dusseldorf can testify. The mystery speaker was unlikely to still be living, but his computer might be recoverable.

Anyway, I made what arrangements I could to enter the Hot Zone, including arranging the pass needed to enter the restricted area with the help of old BBC contacts. Waiting for me at the barrier across the old M11 which was the official way into the Hot Zone was none other than Ken Strike. He was sitting in an ex-military jeep and cradling an AK 47 and a portable Geiger counter. He was just as bearded as ever. He suggested that he should accompany me into the Hot Zone. When I objected, he told me that he was an intelligence services operator and that his accompanying me was non-negotiable. I shrugged; rumour had it that the Hot Zone was dangerous. Having Ken and his paraphernalia along might be useful.

'We know who you're looking for,' Ken told me as I climbed into the jeep.

'That's more than I do,' I replied. 'All I have is an email and an actual address. I call him Arthur.'

Ken drew in his breath sharply. 'How did you know that?'

'Know what?'

'That his code name's Arthur.'

'Listen, I had no idea that MI5 had given him a code name, and certainly didn't know it was Arthur. It's just what I decided to call him. It's a coincidence.'

'I don't believe in coincidences,' Ken snarled. The jeep lurched forward and onto the pitted tarmac beyond the barrier.

The jeep had a radio and since this was better than listening to Ken's icy silence, I tuned into Radio Two. The main news item was that the Thames Barrier had just been closed to protect London from flooding. No one knew when it could be opened again. Ken sniggered and pressed the accelerator. The jeep's engine roared drowning the angry clicking of the Geiger counter.

Soon we arrived at what was left of the address, a pile of rubble less than two metres high. Ken started digging around, fragments of broken brick landed in stagnant pools, spraying fetid water everywhere. With some glee he pulled out a black bag. He passed it to me. The zip was stuck, and I had to cut the bag open. The laptop was still inside and there was the power cable and a mouse in the bag's pocket.

'It should still work,' Ken told me. 'Arthur's computer used RAM only. It doesn't have a hard drive.'

I stuffed the computer and the black bag in my backpack.

'I'll take it back to London; the battery's bound to be knackered.'

Ken nodded. 'Arthur used two computers,' he said. 'A laptop for communication and a secure desktop for other purposes. My bosses want the desktop, we've already got what's on the laptop. Arthur believed that any computer connected to the internet was insecure. He was right of course. Arthur never connected his desktop to the internet. It caused us many headaches.'

When I got back to my rather expensive house in

Richmond, I noticed that the Thames was higher than I'd ever seen it. The first thing I did was turn on the news. A government minister was assuring us that the Thames Barrier had been designed to protect London from flooding. The barrier was now closed. London had been successfully protected. The fact that the barrier could never be opened again was immaterial. True, ships could no longer visit the Port of London, but as none did anyway, the Barrier closing was irrelevant to trade.

Also, he was keen to point out, it was a far-sighted Conservative government who had installed the Thames Barrier in the first place, and at reduced cost.

It took a moment to check. What the minister had said was absolutely true. The massive pumps that were designed to empty the Thames over the barrier had been deleted from the design to save money. If they were needed in the future, say if the barrier were to be closed permanently, they could be retrofitted.

Fuming at the incompetency of politicians, I turned my attention to Arthur's laptop. I discovered his email account quite quickly but couldn't access it. None of the emails were actually stored on the laptop, but on a server somewhere in the US. I would have to hack Arthur's password. This was harder than I anticipated, and I had to resort to some software, developed by the Israelis, but beloved of investigative journalists the world over.

Whilst the software was running, I poked around in the laptop to see what else I could find.

There was an entry for something called the Cambridge Writers' Short Story Competition 2023. The entry was my vlog. I didn't know whether to laugh, cry, or just surrender to madness. The ending was singularly depressing.

Once I'd cracked Arthur's password, the rest was easy. The tip off had been correct. Back in 2022, Arthur had demonstrated that even if the world had gone carbon neutral at that time, then temperatures would still rise to 1.7 degrees above 1850 average, though this would not occur until 2040 at the earliest. He had compared it to switching on a kettle. It won't boil at once but takes several minutes to reach boiling point. The earth is much bigger than a kettle and takes decades to warm. Arthur also noted that it was then still possible to prevent temperatures reaching plus 1.5 degrees. All that was needed was to remove 400 billion tonnes of carbon dioxide from the atmosphere by 2030. Instead, we had all swallowed the lies.

I had planned to end my vlog here, but I've just deleted the final paragraph, so I can tell you what happened in the last few minutes. I was just off to the pub, but when I opened my front door, my attention was grabbed by the ducks swimming where the path should be. The Thames lapping gently at my doorstep was strangely relaxing at one level but in my mind I could hear the screams of men, women and children drowning as the river poured into the London Underground.

The Lost Art of Polydamna

Harry Goode

A man of about fifty, with slumped shoulders and a shuffling gait, arrived at the House of Healing in Corinth. He was accompanied by a young woman, tall and slender, with her shawl wrapped about her head, so as to render the face all but invisible.

Antiphon welcomed the man and led him into an inner chamber. The woman remained in the outer courtyard. She seated herself against the wall and rested her hands on her knees.

'Tell me,' said Antiphon, 'why have you come here?'

'I have heard,' replied the man, 'that you claim you can cure all griefs.'

'That is indeed the case. Many people have arrived here deeply unhappy at the loss of parents, or lovers, or a wife, or children. Always they have left filled with that calm cheerfulness which is becoming to us. Tell me, what loss have you suffered?'

'It's not a loss – not that simple – well, I did lose my wife, but that was nearly eighteen years ago. She died of a fever shortly after the birth of my daughter. She is the one who came here with me today. No, it's not a loss – but it feels like a loss. I wake early every day – before dawn – and it descends on me like a cloud. Despair – that's the only word for it – despair, black despair.'

'And do you know why you have this feeling?'

'No. It has come upon me like an illness. I don't want to engage in any of my usual pursuits. If it weren't for the care of my daughter, all my affairs would be in ruin, my slaves would have made off with all my goods and my life would have ended miserably. And I don't know why – that's the worst thing – I don't know why.'

'I have had such cases before, and you will be glad to know that I have always been successful. However, I think it only fair to warn you that finding a cure is not a simple matter and may take some time. This does, of course, render the treatment more expensive and you must be willing to follow my instruction precisely.'

'Believe me; I would do anything – anything! I have felt like this for over six months and some days I wish to die.'

Antiphon crossed the room to where various plants were growing in pots. He plucked three pale purple blooms from one, crushed the leaves lightly in a mortar and added some wine. He decanted the wine into a small amphora and sealed it with a stopper.

'I am sure you will recall how Homer recounts the visit that Telemachus, son of Odysseus, makes to the court of Menelaus. When they converse, they are overcome with sadness at the thought that Odysseus may have perished. Helen uses the drug Nepenthe to soothe away these sorrows, an art she had learned from the Egyptian woman Polydamna. The Egyptians were the most skilled of all people in the herbal arts.

I wish I had Polydamna's art, but in these degenerate times it is lost. I am afraid I have to apply makeshifts. Just before bedtime, pour a little of this on the ground and drink the rest – in one draught mind you – as a toast to Asclepius. Then I want you to come here early in the day and tell me of any dreams you may have had. Since dreams easily blow away on the morning breezes, tell them to your daughter, so that she can remind you on your way here. Do you consent to do this?'

When they returned to the outer courtyard, the daughter rose to her feet. Antiphon caught a glimpse of one of her eyes. It was a startling green and fringed with dark lashes of remarkable length.

When the pair arrived the next day, the daughter briefly glanced at Antiphon before lowering her eyes and taking up her seat in the courtyard. The man seemed paler than the day before and Antiphon noticed that he had a sword strapped to his side.

'I see that you have dreamt,' opened Antiphon, 'and that this dream has disturbed you. Tell me what happened.'

'A terror – a great terror! I dreamt I was making my way along dark passages. They were damp and I could feel the moisture as I brushed against the walls. It was dark, but somehow I could see where I was going. I knew I was making my way towards something terrible – I didn't know what. I was grasping a sword tightly in one hand. It was my only protection. Then I could hear it – at first like the wind soughing over dark waters – then, like the breathing of a great animal. I knew that round the next bend there was something, something I had to face. I wanted to run but couldn't. The creature was approaching the corner – the sound grew louder – in a moment I would be face to face with it. There was a great clatter. I realized in horror that I had dropped my sword. There was a silence and then I knew it would be upon me and I was helpless. I woke, covered in sweat and found the first light was entering my chamber. I must have lashed out in my sleep, for the lamp had been knocked to the floor and had broken. It seemed so real, more real than any dream I have ever had. This morning I saw the man in the marketplace who offers to interpret dreams. He is there every day and I have heard him spoken of highly. I told him my dream and asked him its meaning. He told me it signifies that I am to have an encounter with an enemy and must make sure I am prepared. That is why you see me armed, although, to be truthful, I cannot imagine who this enemy might be.'

The man hesitated a moment and then continued. 'I did wonder if the enemy could be you, but when I put this to my daughter she laughed and told me that you had a very honest face, and I could be sure that you were not this unknown enemy.'

'Your daughter is perceptive but obviously this market-place dream interpreter is a very learned man. I must make his acquaintance someday. Tell me, you have been a widower for a long time – eighteen years I think you said – have you ever thought of remarrying?'

'No. I had the care and responsibility for my daughter and, as I'm sure you know, stepmothers can be unkind. Now she is grown, she is like a wife to me. She runs the household and looks after my needs. Better than a wife, for she places no demands on me. She has a very sweet and kind nature.'

'You should give thanks to the gods for granting you such a daughter. Meantime, I shall prepare you another draught and want you to come again tomorrow with details of the dream you will have.'

In the outer courtyard, the daughter again gazed at

Antiphon with eyes green as the olive leaf in spring. The rest of her face was covered, but Antiphon had the distinct impression that she was smiling at him.

The following day the man recounted his dream: 'I and my daughter were seated in the open-air eating from a large pot she had prepared. Overhead a hawk was circling round us. I reached out my ladle into the pot and then, to my great horror, I saw that there were human parts floating in the mess – a finger and an ear. I looked up at my daughter and she burst out laughing. In some ways this dream was more terrible than the first. This morning I could not eat the food my daughter had prepared. When she asked me if I had dreamt, I lied and said 'No'. On the way I stopped to ask the market man the meaning. He said that there was no need to fear my daughter; that she was probably laughing because the plot had been foiled. He said it was now clear that my enemy would try to poison me, and I must be sure not to touch anything that had not been prepared by my daughter. Then I told my daughter the dream and the interpretation. I suggested to her that I shouldn't take any more of these preparations you give me. She told me that she would hang herself if she had judged you wrongly, but she thought I should place myself entirely in your hands. That is why I am here again. But I have to say that I cannot see how all these disturbing dreams are helping me. What good can they possibly do?'

'Remarkable! Remarkable prescience!' said Antiphon as he went to his plants and picked three more pale purple flowers. 'Have patience with my methods, they always work eventually – and do please take any more dreams you have to the market man. I must make the effort of going to him myself.'

When they went to the outer courtyard, the daughter was looking away from them. The side of her face was uncovered, and Antiphon could see a pale white neck, over which curled fine dark hair. A large gold ring hung from the delicately shaped ear. As she turned towards them, she covered her face slowly.

The next day, the girl kept her face uncovered as her father greeted Antiphon. She had high cheek bones and full lips of a soft pink hue. Her skin was translucent and seemed to be covering the faint beginnings of a blush.

The man seemed lighthearted. 'I dreamt,' he said, 'once again of my daughter. She was standing looking out to sea. There was a boat with white sails some way off. I approached her from behind and placed my hand on her shoulder. At that moment she changed into a golden statue. She could neither move nor speak. I felt overcome with sadness. When I told her about the dream, she just said that she would rather be a gold statue than an iron one. The man in the marketplace was very reassuring. He said that the dream augured that my daughter would remain like gold to me and look after me into old age. This has left me feeling cheerful.'

'Clearly a man who knows his craft to its very depths. This man deserves a state office. He is a veritable Calchas come back to life – and to think that we can find him in our very own marketplace! Tell me, has your daughter no suitors?'

The man flushed angrily. 'Of course she has. I always send them away wishing that they hadn't bothered asking. My daughter, like her mother, is a great beauty. The sort of dogs you find around here aren't fit to walk in her shadow.'

'Clearly the gods who took your wife left something equally valuable. Have you asked her how she feels about these things?'

'She tells me she is happy to respect my wishes. But what has all this got to do with effecting a cure for me?'

'You are right; we should stick to the task in hand. Be patient; I have not forgotten. You have done every day exactly as I have asked you. I can only guarantee your cure if you will now obey my further instructions.'

The man hesitated, but finally agreed.

'Good. Now, here in Corinth there is a beautiful widow, quite wealthy too. I have already spoken to her about you, and she has observed your passages to and from here through a crack in her shutters. You are going to meet her and offer her marriage.'

The man jumped to his feet.

'What has it got to do with you whether or not I am married? When I look around, I see lots of men who are not particularly happy with their wives. You don't expect me to pay you for such stupid advice?'

'You agreed to adopt the measures I think are necessary for a cure. You are a gentleman, so you must honour your word. But there is a further part of the cure. You will let me marry your daughter. I believe you will find that she will agree to this.'

The man took two paces towards Antiphon.

'You are a scoundrel. If I had my sword with me I would run you through. You have heard me tell of my daughter's good qualities, and now you think you can steal her from me. Never! I say never!'

'When I tell you the meaning of your dreams, the real meaning that is, I'm sure you will agree to both my proposals. Let's take each dream in turn. The maze you dreamt of, where lurked some terrible monster, was none other than the maze of Daedalus – the one he built to house the Minotaur. You will remember, of course, that this creature was the result of an unnatural congress between Pasiphaë, the wife of King Minos, and one of the bulls of Poseidon. This was the first thing that told me that deep in your soul was a fear of some unspeakable act – an act of the kind that brings down the retribution of the gods. Now, your second dream. Your daughter serves you a meal that contains parts of a dismembered body. You will recall how Clymeneus wickedly forced his daughter Harpalyce. She then took her revenge by killing her younger brother and serving his cut up flesh to her father. In case you doubt this is the true meaning, consider how the gods turned Harpalyce into a hawk. There was a hawk in your dream.'

The man had now seated himself again. He had grown very pale.

'When in the third dream you touched your daughter and she turned into gold, this was not as you thought a good omen. Gold is indeed valuable but, as king Midas found, a live daughter is better. This dream warned that if you touch your daughter, touch her that is as fathers should not touch their daughters, then you will kill her. Now, can you see that your three dreams were really just one dream? The gods, or perhaps that part of ourselves we call our conscience, was telling you that you harboured wrongful desires for your daughter. She is beautiful. She reminds you of your dead wife. That is why I have prescribed a remedy that puts both you and your daughter out of harm's way.'

When they returned to the outer courtyard, the daughter came forward, openly smiling at Antiphon.

I am a Spy

Richard Gould

Together

'There's something I need to tell you, Dean.'

'Tell me later, Stace. I'm watching this.'

'I want to tell you now.'

'Why've you muted it?'

'Because I want you to listen to me.'

'OK, I am listening but make it quick, 'cos I can't hear what they're saying.'

'That's because I've put it on mute.'

'I know that; I'm not stupid. I didn't mean I can't hear it; I meant I want to hear it.' They were sitting together on the sofa in the living room. Stacey had taken possession of the remote.

'Now what?' Dean protested.

'I've switched it off because you were still watching, and I want your undivided attention. You can catch up on iPlayer later.'

'Well, I've got no choice have I? I'm all ears. What's so important that Eastenders has to wait?'

'I'm a spy.'

'Fine. Can you switch it back on now?'

'Did you hear what I said? I'm a spy.'

'If you won't, then hand me the remote.'

'Aren't you going to ask me about it?'

'You want me to believe you're a spy? Come on love, switch it back on.'

'I pass messages on at the dry cleaners. I've been doing it for almost a year now.'

'Messages? What sort of messages?'

'I'm not allowed to read them, everything's sealed. Sometimes they're those little sticks that fit into a computer.'

'Chopsticks!'

'Not funny, you know the ones I mean, they have information on them.'

'And who has got you to do all this spying, Stace? The Prime Minister? Or is it King Charles?'

'That's the problem, he's not English. He seemed nice enough at first, but I think I'm spying for bad people.'

'Well, I suggest you stop it then. Please put the telly back on.'

Stacey

Stacey worked at a dry cleaners in a posh part of the city, the sort of neighbourhood where people were too lazy to even wash and iron their own shirts. It was a busy place, men in suits coming in early morning and late afternoon, women handing in designer label dresses and jackets during the day. Sometimes the women didn't look like they were rich, and they didn't speak posh either. Maybe they were housekeepers or nannies Stacey thought.

She recognised some of the regulars including the one who looked like Sean Connery in the Raiders of the Lost Ark films when he was Harrison Ford's dad – tall, upright, quite fanciable despite his age. He was as polite as hell, always with a 'Good morning' and a friendly smile. Sometimes he handed over a tenner tip when he collected his clothes.

One morning he brought in a flat white coffee and a Pret Bar. 'For you,' he announced with one of those nice smiles as he handed them over.

'They're my favourites.'

'Of course!'

'But how do you know? You ain't been watching me, have you?'

There was no immediate answer and Stacey wondered whether he was a pervert. Nevertheless, when he extended his arm, she grabbed hold and they shook hands. 'Alexsei Mikhailov.'

'Stacey Russell.'

'A pleasure to meet you, Stacey Russell.'

With a name like his Stacey expected an accent, but there was none. He spoke proper Queen's English – or was it now King's English she wondered. She could never like Camilla, not after what had happened to Lady Di.

Mr Mikhailov turned up a couple of times a week, usually around when a coffee and snack wouldn't go amiss. He stayed on to chat as she drank her flat white and ate the snack bar. He was so busy asking her questions, about what she liked doing in her spare time, her family and friends, that she had no opportunity to find out anything about him.

It was a Friday morning, the first day that felt springlike with a warm sun. The plant containers outside were bursting with daffodils. Mr Mikhailov asked Stacey something that she was uncomfortable answering, what with Dean ‘between jobs’ as he called it and her work at the dry cleaners paying lousy wages. They were strapped for cash.

So, when he asked, 'Do you have enough money to lead a comfortable life?' she burst into tears.

Mr Mikhailov produced a polka dot handkerchief from his jacket breast pocket and handed it over. Checking that it was unused, Stacey dabbled her eyes before passing it back. 'It seems, not enough money,' the man said. He appeared to be in deep thought before continuing. 'I think I can help you.'

Oh yeah, was Stacey’s immediate thought. You dirty sod, you want my knickers down. 'There are people I need to communicate with but being foreign it is best not done through the usual channels. If I paid you for passing on messages, would you be interested?'

You’re gay and you don’t want it out in public, Stacey was thinking. Meet me in the public toilets behind Chelsea Town Hall, stuff like that. If that was his thing, then so what? She had an LGBT+ badge (admittedly never worn) so it wasn’t as if she minded gays. Dean didn’t know but she’d had sex with a girlfriend in her late teens.

'I might be interested,' she said.

'All you need do is take something out of a pocket from whatever I’ve handed in to be cleaned and put it in someone else's garment. You would have to be a hundred percent certain that it went to the right person.'

'I would be careful, but ...'

'You are thinking why I want this secrecy and how much will I pay you?'

'The why is none of my business really.'

'You would get £500 – in cash – for each message exchange.'

Stacey was speechless. Stacey was rarely speechless. She'd been thinking that she would do the message exchange for anything over £50 a time. The sum Mr Mikhailov mentioned had left her gobsmacked.

'Why not have a think about it and let me know your decision the next time I'm in? You do need to be aware of one thing though before deciding. If you accept, it has to be done in utmost secrecy. Even this conversation must remain between the two of us.'

Stacey was good at keeping secrets. She hadn't told her parents for months after she'd quit college and started working. She hadn't told her boyfriend Raz that she was seeing Dean. She hadn't told Dean, well, lots of things that he didn't need to know.

'My lips are sealed,' Stacey said as she pretended to run a zip across her mouth before opening it wide to take a bite of her Pret Bar.

A nanny-housekeeper had come into the shop carrying a bin bag full of clothes. 'I'll leave you to it,' Mr Mikhailov said and left.

The woman emptied the bag onto the counter without

an acknowledgement or a word. Stacey began to sort the clothes. 'Lovely day at last, isn't it?' she said with a smile that wasn't reciprocated. These women were snootier than their bosses.

Mr Mikhailov was back the next morning.

'I accept your offer,' Stacey told him.

'I'm pleased. Lord Rigby has a Saville Row suit with you, I believe. A navy pin stripe. He'll be collecting it today and I'd like you to put this envelope in his inside jacket pocket.' Mikhailov handed Stacey two envelopes, the second one bulging and sealed with Sellotape. 'This one is for you.'

As soon as he had left Stacey did as instructed before ripping open the second envelope. It was filled with twenty-pound notes. Instinct told her that there was no need to count: she could trust Mr Mikhailov.

She knew who Lord Rigby was and didn't like him. He was pompous with a voice to go with it and was always looking at her tits rather than her face when handing things in. Mind you, she'd got it wrong if he was gay, unless he was one of those bi people.

Minutes after Mr Mikhailov had departed the Lord was in, taking his suit carefully wrapped in a protective cover, paying by card, and leaving without making eye contact. As soon as Stacey's shift was over, she raced across to the bank over the road and opened an account to deposit the money. It wasn't exactly going to be a secret, but since Dean mustn't know about the messaging service it would be difficult to explain a money windfall. Maybe, later on, she could announce a lottery win.

Over the following months she was to see Mr Mikhailov

many times. Sometimes he would hand over a £50 note in addition to the fat envelope, its contents dispatched immediately to the bank unless a dress or pair of shoes had taken her fancy at Jigsaw, Hobbs or Le La Boutique, these having replaced M&S and H&M now that she was cash rich. Dean didn't notice the upgrade in quality; she hadn't expected him to. However, he would question her ability to afford the holiday break to Dubai that she had booked for them when winter was at its worst.

Stacey was good at making things up. She dropped down next to Dean on the sofa, setting a beer for him and a glass of bubbly for her onto the coffee table. 'Remember my aunt in Newcastle?' she said. 'Well, she died, and she's left me a dollop of money.'

'Wait a sec, there's less than five minutes to go. We need a win.'

'This is more important than football.'

Dean looked as if she had said the most outrageous thing possible. 'I don't know what your 'this' is, do I? Christ, they've scored. Sod it.'

For an instant Stacey considered going on holiday without Dean, but with the match over she announced how she intended to spend a part of the inheritance and he seemed happy enough.

They had a great time away, their first holiday abroad for years, and in such a lavish hotel and luxurious resort.

'Did you enjoy your holiday,' Mr Mikhailov asked on her return to the dry cleaners, the designer label outfit and intense tan suggesting that she had.

The messaging to-and-fro resumed as frequently as

ever. Lord Rigby. A bishop. An actress. Someone from the government who she'd seen interviewed on TV. A foreign footballer in the team Dean supported.

And the money kept rolling in.

Dean

When Stacey announced that she was a spy Dean's first thought was 'here we go again'.

His wife was a pathological liar. It hadn't taken long for him to realise that was the case. When they first met at that Soho nightclub, all those years ago, she'd spoken with a foreign accent, telling him that she was a princess from a country she had best not name.

His suspicion was immediately aroused when she took him back to her flat that evening; it was hardly a place fit for a princess. The bedsit was in a dismal part of the city and the furnishings had seen far better days, including the lumpy mattress they had sex on.

'I thought princesses were rich,' he dared to suggest the following morning as they munched supermarket own brand cornflakes sloshed down with instant coffee.

'I had to flee my country before I was imprisoned.' The accent had changed from East Europeanish to Indianish and was to change again later that morning to Cockney. As they chatted about their lives the impossibilities piled up. She had survived a plane crash in the Alps, sustained by melting and drinking snow until the rescue, days later. An assassin had been foiled by her escape between hotel balconies.

Her lies were so blatantly obvious Dean wondered why she bothered with them. Having headed home after that first day together, he was on the internet. Mythomania, he discovered it was called, lying with no end purpose. This woman either actually believed she was telling the truth, or was lying to make her life seem more exciting than it really was.

All those years ago and they were still together because Stace was a stunner, fabulous in bed, and if you let the lies pass you by, loads of fun. The only difficult times were when she was off on one in front of friends, and he had to keep schtum.

A spy at the dry cleaners! Yeah, sure.

Together

'I want to stop spying, Dean, but I can't. I asked him but he won't let me.'

'He? Who's the he?'

'Mr Mikhailov.'

Dean remembered something Stace had said during their holiday in Dubai. 'Listen Dean. This is top secret, but Auntie Flo is actually Alexsei Mikhailov.' She was on a sunbed knocking back her fourth or fifth cocktail at the time, so Dean hadn't taken much notice.

'I'm sure you can stop being a spy, Stace. There's nothing to worry about.'

'The name, Dean. Mikhailov? Russia? Invasion of Ukraine? The nuclear bomb threat?' Stacey's lies were usually about mundane, personal things. Dean was impressed that she had begun to take an interest in world events. Maybe in her head she could sort out the North Korea danger.

'I'm sure it'll all blow over, Stace.'

'When I told Mikhailov that was it, he said stopping wasn't an option. Hard luck, I said, because I'm quitting. Do you know what he did?'

'Strictly is about to start. You like that so why don't we watch it and you can tell me everything later.'

'He came right up close, our faces almost touching. His smile had gone, his eyes were icy and piecing. 'How's Dean getting on with the new job. It's quite a commute he's got from your lovely little house every day, isn't it.' That's what he said. He knows where we live and where you work.'

'Hand me the remote.'

'I'm scared, Dean. Do you know what his last words were this morning? 'My dear, I can't let you stop because you know too much. And as for your handsome Dean, I'm assuming he knows all about our arrangement. too.''

The doorbell chimed and Stacey flinched.

'Who can that be?' Dean said as he stood up.

Stacey grabbed hold of his leg. 'Don't answer it.'

Dean pulled free of her grip. 'Don't be silly.'

'I'm calling the police.'

Dean was by the living room door. 'Enough, Stace, enough.'

'He’s out to kill us.'

'No worries. This’ll be the Prime Minister or King Charles paying us a visit! Or maybe both of them. You’d better put the kettle on.'

Dean was still laughing as he opened the front door.

Stacey was crying.

What did you do in the war, Daddy?

Christine Hawkes

Michael Shaw pulled aside the blackout curtain to gaze at the December moon. His eye fell on the tranquil indigo fields beyond the vegetable patch. No flashes, bangs or distant fires. The horror reported daily from Europe and beyond also infected British lives. Luckily for him, only his beloved rose garden perished: usurped by a corrugated metal air-raid shelter.

'Close the curtain,' called his wife Barbara, titivating in the bathroom. 'With that light on, we'll be a good target for Jerry.' She returned to the bedroom and smiled at her reflection in the dressing table mirror, moving closer with a frown at a red blotch. 'Shall I cut my hair, Mike?'

Several friends had the new, short hairdos. Despite the war, she still looked smart, saving her clothing coupons like a squirrel.

'You know what I think,' he responded. Barbara would please herself.

Michael perused the headlines of the News Chronicle while eating breakfast with bulletins on the wireless blasting the latest news from the front. He sighed. 'John said his conscription papers had arrived.' Barbara knew his colleague, a Freemason, and she dismissed him as 'just part of an old boys' club'. Given the chance, she would have loved to hobnob with the smarter wives at the Lodge. 'I'm seriously thinking of joining up, Bar.' At which point their young son Robin, followed by twin Susan, barged in.

'Super, Daddy! You'll be in uniform. Will you fly planes?'

he demanded, as he zoomed round the kitchen table with arms outstretched.

'Sit down at once and eat your porridge, young man!' Glaring at her son, his mother attempted to eat some toast, then stopped. 'It's quite preposterous, Mike. Weaving bandages and surgical dressings is vital war work. If you join up, so shall I. The children will be quite safe with my mother.'

Michael stared at her in disbelief.

'You're joking, old girl! You wouldn't survive in the ATS. I work in the office at the mill, not in the weaving sheds. D'you, think I don't get flack?'

Susan looked at the newspaper propped against the tea cosy and pointed. 'What's a con...chie, Dad?'

'A coward!' snapped her mother. Michael wiped his mouth on the Rinso-white napkin, refolding it with great care and said, 'I'll explain later, Susan.' He strode to the hall. Shrugging into his well-worn overcoat and grabbing the brown felt trilby, he left; he closed the door with the quiet control of a determined man and strode to the nearby bus stop.

Later the children left for school, complete with gas masks. Like air raid shelters, any protection seemed simply a good luck charm in the sleepy village. Barbara knew that Michael would remember to tell Susan about the war; he was a man for facts, not fairy stories or half-truths. She surveyed the breakfast table. Not much toast eaten: how could she use it up? Crumble? There were Bramley's stored in the larder. Scrimping, eking things out, she was tired of it. No wonder she had snapped earlier. And why should they suffer on reduced forces pay, when Michael had a valid reason for staying at work? Barbara glanced at the grandfather clock, a relic from Michael's great aunt and felt relieved she was meeting her mother, Diana, at the café. The attractive widow and her daughter had plenty in common, besides stubborn ways and large brown eyes. She could mull things over with the older woman.

Barbara peered through the Bon-Bon café window. There was Diana Blackwell, looking at her watch with a flash of red lacquered nails, her cigarette in a tortoiseshell holder. 'At last!' to the young woman hurrying to her table. She proffered a rouged cheek for her daughter's reddened lips and sniffed. 'Mmm. Blue Grass scent. Lovely.'

'Sorry, Mother. I heard the butcher had some rabbits, but he said I'd heard wrong. I don't believe him.'

'Never mind. Give them cheese on toast. If you haven't used all your cheese ration. Here's something to spoil them.' Diana slid a brown paper bag across the table, 'Ask no questions...' The women ordered coffee and scones, knowing they would arrive with margarine, not butter. Barbara accepted a cigarette, after a moment's hesitation. Michael would disapprove; he liked women to be violet breathed and she usually played along with his notion of her fragrant fragility, though both probably knew it was a sham. Her involuntary sigh raised Diana Blackwell's eyebrows.

'What can possibly be wrong with my girl? An upright, handsome husband, with a good job, two healthy children...'

'He's joining up. And he needn't. Why should we live on

an army pittance? I don't want to be a war widow, like you were, when he's reported missing. Why should Robin and Susan lose their father, like I did? You never said much, but it must have been hard.'

Looking bemused, the older woman took a long pull on the Player's cigarette between her talons. 'Your father wasn't actually... in the services, Babs. He did whatever job he could get in 1914; worked on the railway, anything to avoid being called up. 'Dodging the column' we called it.' Barbara crushed the cigarette into her scone; neither appealed now.

'I was born in Manchester in 1915... when did you get married? You were married?' Her wide hazel eyes fixed the older woman's narrowed chestnut ones, who responded, biting her lip.

'As soon as he, Roger Morris, realized I had a bun in the oven, he scooted. You might well look sick. Slang for pregnant. With no relatives and a war on, I moved down here to a housekeeper's job. I've brought you up well. You wanted for nothing and you suspected nothing.'

'So... I'm just a bastard? But you certainly encouraged me to think I was somebody special. And I'm not. I didn't have a brave father who was 'missing, presumed dead, while fighting valiantly for his beloved country'. He...buggered off. Because he didn't want me.' Again, brightening eyes held the faded, wrinkling gaze, which lowered first.

'Not a pretty way to talk, Barbara.'

'No. Everything sordid was kept at arm's length. What a gullible fool I've been. I didn't press you for details because you didn't seem to want to discuss him. I allowed you to fill my head with romantic notions about my lost soldier daddy! But it never really added up.' On a whim, Barbara took out a powder compact and checked her eye makeup wasn't smudged. She applied a brave veneer of crimson lipstick to her cupid's bow and stood up. Snapping her bag shut, she pulled on brown leather gloves. 'I must pop into the Ladies and go, Mother. I'm seeing Jenny at the WVS. Thanks for the coffee. Chicory, rather. Roger... how well named! Nothing's ever quite what it seems, is it?'

'Give Michael my love. And congratulations. Your husband has principles, Barbara.'

In the lavatories, Barbara combed her long wavy hair, thinking about her mother. So many things hadn't made sense, but since she had never met her supposed father, she couldn't in all honesty claim many regrets. She had been spared any unpleasant comments at school and, until now, had a confidence built on false pride. She would tell Mike, of course, but he had always seen Diana as 'the merry widow'. Had he suspected more than she had?

Crossing from the Bon-Bon to the WVS headquarters, Barbara nodded to the head scarved women finishing their Woodbines in the doorway. The wives of men who had joined up sometimes did a short stint there. They packed parcels, knitted for the troops, and gossiped, in addition to working shifts at a munitions factory in nearby Kirby. Presumably, their mothers minded any children. Lord Haw Haw might scare some women into believing Hitler would soon invade Britain, but it didn't prevent them working hard for the war effort. Inside the drill hall, 'Workers' Playtime' blasted. Vera Lynn optimistically singing 'We'll meet again' from the wireless. Jenny Porter was there, lifting piles of woollen clothing onto a large sheet of brown paper, her halo of hair flattened beneath her hat. She looked up with surprise, at Barbara's approach.

'Come in here,' she mouthed, and led her into a side room. 'Did Michael tell you? About the vile letter?' Barbara shook her head. 'You know that picture of John in the local rag for good works at the Lodge? Some rotter cut it out and sent it to him with...with...'

'With what?'

'They had wiped their bottom on the photo. And scrawled 'conchie' across a piece of Izal paper.'

'But he's not! He does legitimate war work!' Barbara was indignant.

'You know, I know, but most men are away on active service. You must have noticed we don't get many friendly looks round the village, now. Anyway, he's joining up. He had felt he should, and I won't stop him.' She sighed.

'Come and meet the others; you will see there is so much to do here.'

Barbara following Jenny, was amazed at the activity in the bigger, church hall. Women were knitting woollen scarves and vests, sewing pyjamas, sorting clothing into different piles for men, women, children and babies. At another table, dolls' houses, railway sets, boxes of games, skipping ropes and spinning tops were being examined for salvaging and passing on. 'You didn't know all this was happening? Children are evacuated here because it's safer than the cities and if they were bombed, they'd have few belongings and resources. We need all the help we can get, Barbara.'

Once at home, Barbara pondered over the day, pulling dark velvet curtains across the bay window. She paused. Not to admire her reflection, but in awe at the purple blue twilight. 'Slowly, silently, now the moon…' Walter De La Mare's poem, from primary school, she remembered and looked at the garden and the apple tree, bathed in silver. How easy it had been to believe in calm and peace, here. Yet, what were some people in the village thinking about them? No wonder the butcher was 'hiding' his rabbits. She felt hot with shame. Her mother had tried to make her daughter's life as pleasant as she could, shielded from reality. Now she was on Mike's side. And there was Jenny: not worrying about herself but prepared for her husband to join up. It was a confusing time. How could it be thought worse to have a conscience about warfare and killing, than to dodge the war for selfish, cowardly reasons? She was glad she had changed into a pretty new dress, to cheer Michael up after being cross at breakfast. She must remember she'd had it for ages if he asked.

Raised voices from the children squabbling over snakes and ladders distracted Barbara and the squeak of the front door opening produced a shout from Susan, 'Daddy!' She raced to hug her father while Peter deftly moved her red counter on the board before following. Since Michael was home early, they listened to Children's Hour together. It was a welcome distraction from the mood at breakfast, with information about nature, and the listeners' responses to the young princesses' broadcast earlier in the week.

Michael looked at his wife and smiled. 'The corned beef was a treat – never mind rabbit. And how was the fair Diana?'

'Oh! I forgot. Bring my handbag, Susan. Granny sent something.'

Barbara withdrew the paper bag and the children pounced. 'Chocolate! Fry's! Where did she find it?'

Michael frowned. 'Not more Black Market, Barbara? She could be fined. Even sent to prison...'

'Where's the black market, Daddy? I've never seen it.' Peter was interested. Barbara sighed. Not the day to share the news with Michael that her father, if he were her father, hadn't been a war casualty after all. Perhaps she would just forget about it, for a while. She told them about the wonderful work being done by village volunteers to provide for any evacuees who might come for safety from the big cities. And she was going to help them, and the soldiers fighting, too.

'Could you spare some of your toys and books for the children?'

'Oh yes! Just like Princess Elizabeth said, Mummy ....'

Barbara wasn't really listening. She was pleased she had kept her hair longer: it would look very attractive under a WVS hat.

The Eulogist

Quintin Langley-Coleman

There was a knock.

Henry Merriweather started as if he had received many volts and glanced askance at the door. Clients were uncommon – unsurprising for a poet-for-hire – and Merriweather had a briny disposition, so shocks came easily to him. Another knock, and Merriweather fumbled to gather and neaten the pencils and papers splayed across his desk. A third knock came, this one firmer and faster than the prior two. Merriweather sensed impatience and irritation; the mess would have to wait. 'Come in!'

The door opened and in strode a well-groomed, middle-aged man wearing a pale grey greatcoat and gloves, ahead of whom wafted a cosy ripple of cologne.

'Cold, isn't it?' said the man, peeling off his coat and gloves and hanging them on the back of the door.

Merriweather looked out the window at the warm sunshine streaming in. 'Looks rather warm actually, but I've been inside all morning so perhaps it's colder than it seems.'

'Doubt it,' said the man firmly, 'It's just the contrast. I was in the Serengeti on a hunt before being called back for... well, you know.'

Merriweather certainly did not know, and not wanting to appear foolish decided to approach the matter indirectly, 'Erm, what was your name again?'

'Krummholtz von Wintergarten,' said the man, 'Were

you not expecting me?' Von Wintergarten looked about the room, taking it in for the first time. 'No, I suppose not. I spoke with your secretary, you know.'

'Pilkins?' asked Merriweather, surprised.

Pilkins was an out-of-work actor friend of his who sometimes pretended to be Merriweather's business partner, and had drummed up a few clients for him in this way; but Pilkins had never pretended to be his secretary before.

'I don't recall,' said von Wintergarten, 'I'm no good with names. I was given the form, but I haven't had time to fill it out, and my handwriting is botched anyway, so I'm here now to go through it all with you. Didn't your secretary say?'

Merriweather shook his head.

'Ah, well, we choose them for looking at and not thinking anyway.'

Merriweather made a noncommittal noise as he swallowed a kernel of immediate dislike; and mustering his calm said, 'Mister von Wintergarten, what exactly are you here for?'

Von Wintergarten's expression turned dark and beety.

'Look chum, what the bloody hell do you think I'm here for?' he roared, and Merriweather jumped back, 'I am the client, I'm bloody paying you, and let me tell you I'm bloody busy! You, you—'

Then suddenly he stopped his tirade as quickly as it had begun, and a knowing grin stole across his face. 'Ah,' he said, 'I see what you're doing. You want me to just come out with it, eh? To articulate the, ah, situation so that I fully accept it, hmm?' Merriweather hesitated, then nodded once, very slowly.

'Well,' said von Wintergarten, now placid as an unruffled lake, 'I'm not the sentimental type. My father, Feldspar von Wintergarten, died and so I've had to cut short my hunting trip and trudge back here to do the bloody funeral speech. However,' and here he sneered, 'I do not love words and I did not love my father, so I thought I'd come to you – highly recommended as you are – to commission you to write it for me.' Silence reigned.

Von Wintergarten rubbed his hands together. 'Yes, that felt rather good.' He looked at Merriweather. 'You're looking rather pale, chum. Are you not the ew-low-gist?' Merriweather drew in a deep breath to prepare to explain three things to Krummholtz von Wintergarten. First, the correct pronunciation is yoo-logist. Second, he is not a eulogist but rather an elegist. And third, it is not polite to refer to a recent acquaintance as 'chum'. However, such things were to remain unsaid, for von Wintergarten went on, 'For three thousand pounds, you'd better be!'

'Three thousand pounds?' Merriweather's desire to correct von Wintergarten melted away.

'Right here, indeed,' said von Wintergarten, pulling out an envelope that was plump and straining from the bulk of cash within.

'And, uh, for what length of speech?'

'I thought I'd leave that up to you, being the expert ew-low-gist and all. Not too short lest I appear uncaring, nor too long – no one likes a droner at a funeral. They're so glum already! Maybe two to five minutes?'

Merriweather did some mental arithmetic, and at its conclusion felt a warmth seeping into his body, as though he had drunk whisky. He nodded vigorously. 'Yes, yes, that's eminently doable.' 'Brill,' said von Wintergarten, 'Let's rampage through this questionnaire, then—' he pulled out a folded paper from his pocket, '—as I'm off for a pre-lunch squash match with the vicar.'

Merriweather grabbed a pencil and scrap of paper, and motioned for von Wintergarten to read. Von Wintergarten unfolded the paper and squinted hard. It was clear that reading provided an equal (if not greater) challenge than a Serengeti expedition, and he enunciated the words with slow deliberation. 'Describe. The deceased. In three phrases. As honestly. As you can.'

Von Wintergarten looked up. 'Well, that's easy enough: he loved himself; he loved animals, especially killing them; and he loved not spending time with his family – thank goodness – preferring to gamble, drink, snort, and shoot.'

'Snort?' asked Merriweather.

'Don't be dim, doctor. I'm talking about non-medicinal substances.' He paused. 'Well?'

'Well, what?'

'Did I answer that question correctly?'

Merriweather forced a smile. 'You certainly answered it honestly. However, it might need some dressing up. Instead of 'self-love', let's say 'confidence'; instead of 'killing animals', let's say he 'enjoyed the great outdoors'; and instead of 'drink and snort', we might say your father 'enjoyed life to the fullest'.'

Von Wintergarten furrowed his brow in thought.

Merriweather's heart thundered in his chest, afraid, though not exactly sure what he was afraid of. Then von Wintergarten's features softened, and he smiled.

'That's very clever! Ha! Very clever indeed. I knew you were the man for the job.'

Now it was Merriweather's turn for his features to soften and to smile. 'Shall we do question two?'

They continued in this way until the questionnaire had been totally answered, and Merriweather had transmuted the memory of Feldspar von Wintergarten from a narcissistic, cruel, crooked old addict into a selfless, kind, straightlaced young-at-heart man taken too soon from this world to leave behind his doting family and two prized spaniels, Rufus and Tiberius.

Krummholtz von Wintergarten went off to play squash with the vicar. He would come back the next day. Merriweather set to work putting this new memory of the deceased into elegiac couplets immediately, lest he linger upon the fraudulent nature of his undertaking. He could always rationalize it post-hoc.

***

A week later, Merriweather was pacing his office. He had penned the poem for von Wintergarten in a single sitting, achieving a state of near bliss as the words flowed out of him. It transpired that three thousand pounds was an excellent motivator, and couplet by elegiac couplet he painted a false but beautiful picture of Feldspar von Wintergarten; so much so that he even felt an inkling of admiration himself for this man he had never met. At its end, his cheeks were flush with accomplishment, and he prepared a copy for von Wintergarten. Von Wintergarten came the next day, complaining of someone being a 'shivering wetty' (whatever that was – Merriweather was disinclined to inquire) and took the elegy without casting the faintest glance over it. Merriweather had entreated him to do so, but von Wintergarten had been in a rush to another sporting event and had parted expressing his having the highest confidence in his ew-low-gist.

It was at the exact moment when Merriweather saw his office door close behind the departing von Wintergarten that a gust of worry curled across his skin like a draught across uneven floorboards. He feared his fraud being discovered. He worried that he might have given von Wintergarten the wrong paper. He felt burdened that someone would have such effortless confidence him in; dreaded how the poem might be received; and anguished that he might never find out. All these sentiments formed a chemical cocktail within him, each rationalisation dissolving one anxiety but precipitating another and so on without end.

And so, Merriweather paced his office while that plump envelope of three thousand pounds lay untouched in his desk drawer. He did not know when the funeral was to take place or whether it had already taken place, and added to his inner tumult the idle question of how long one must be anxious for before one's heart exploded. He would never discover the answer to that question, however, for at that moment there was a knock at the door.

Merriweather yelped and stopped pacing. No other

knocks came, and instead the door swung open and in strode Krummholtz von Wintergarten, his face already dark and beety. His gloved fists were clenching and unclenching as though wringing imaginary necks, and Merriweather fled behind his desk to put an obstacle between himself and what he reckoned was his certain doom.

'I'm not happy,' said von Wintergarten, clearly uninterested in meteorological observations today.

'The eulogy didn't go down well, then?' said Merriweather lightly.

'The what?'

'The... the funeral speech.'

'Ah, no. It went down well, actually.'

'Oh?' Merriweather was pleased at this, but the ferocity of von Wintergarten's expression allowed no room for solace.

'Indeed, everyone afterwards congratulated me on how brilliant and moving it was. But,' and here von Wintergarten sneered and Merriweather's mind was filled with images of cold iron bars 'the worst, most unforgivable thing was that they told me it was terribly poetic.'

Merriweather blinked. 'Is that so bad?'

'Of course, it is!' roared von Wintergarten, 'You made me look like a shivering wetty, you snake! I had told you I had about as little love for words as I did my father, and now all and sundry think I love both and it's your fault. Bah! Me! A poet! What on earth would make them think that?'

'Did you not notice that the speech rhymed?'

'I just read the speech aloud. I didn't have time to notice anything about it,' said von Wintergarten with venom. He took a deep breath. 'Now, something needs to be done.'

'Of course, of course,' said Merriweather, fetching the envelope from his desk and proffering it forward. 'Anyone unhappy with my work gets a full refund, of course.'

'I think we're beyond refunds, don't you?' said von Wintergarten, pulling off his gloves. The envelope in Merriweather's outstretched hand started flapping like a leaf in a storm.

'Please,' Merriweather said, 'I'll do anything. I'll even go to the police and turn myself in.'

'Turn yourself in for what?' asked von Wintergarten, peeling off his coat and hanging it on the back of the study door.

'For... for, uh, fraud?'

'Ha!' Von Wintergarten laughed. 'Oh, that doesn't bother me. Doesn't bother me at all. We've all committed a spot of fraud here or there, hmm? However, what does bother me is that I must now uphold the pretence of being a poet.'

'If I could—' but von Wintergarten's raised hand stopped Merriweather short.

'What you will do is the following, and I am sure you won't disagree. First, you must get rid of your current clients and take on no future ones.'

Merriweather nodded. This was one of those rare actions that is just as easily said as done.

'Second, you will never speak to anyone ever about this, nor keep any record in any form that concerns your connection to me, my family, or my associates.'

Merriweather nodded. Already he had been too nervous to tell anyone, and certainly would not now.

'Third and last, you shall retain me as your sole and only client – though I shall retain the right to allow your services to individuals I specify – and your services shall consist of teaching me how to 'do poetry' along with commission pieces as and when the need arises.'

Merriweather did not nod. His mind was busy trying to square the circle between the brutalities he imagined he would be subjected to and the words that had just come out of von Wintergarten's mouth.

'You want to... uh, to hire me?'

'Yes, at a small but robust salary, with bonuses for each commission. Seems only fair that, given what you've done to my reputation, I should make sole use of you in maintaining that new reputation.'

Merriweather spoke before his brain knew what his tongue was doing. 'Of course, yes. That strikes me as very fair.'

'Then we are agreed. If you give me something to write with and something to write upon, then we can begin.'

'Begin what?'

'Don't be dim! The lesson, of course! You don't have any other clients anymore, remember?'

Merriweather in a moment of epiphany suddenly realised the changed state of the world and of his role in it. Like removing dark lenses from his eyes, he smiled at a world now bright with promise and possibility.

'Right,' he said, passing a paper and pencil to von Wintergarten, 'Let's start with what a rhyme is, and how to spot one.'

Wildlife

Tim Love

When the quarry closed, Chalk Road became a useless loop off the Bedford bypass. Before work, I'd park up there in a lay-by overlooking the fenced off area. I thought nobody else knew about the lay-by. There was no litter, no bridleway sign. Sue would arrive out of breath, hide her bike behind my car and we'd jump into the back, not even bothering to move the baby-seat. One morning, two old men appeared with cameras. We froze. They seemed to take no notice of us, pausing to sip from their Thermos flasks while talking about the discovery of great crested newts in the quarry. When they disappeared over the barbed wire fence, I wanted to continue but Sue pulled her clothes up and got out. In fairness, she had the most to lose if we were discovered, but I was left frustrated. Unable to find another location, and realising it was only sex that made us bother, we stopped seeing each other outside work.

I'm telling you all this now in case later you think I take advantage of vulnerable women. Sue was my boss's boss, not someone to muck about with. I started jogging into work again and taking early showers. One of the perks of working in a big place was having a little gym on site with showers and free coffee, so it became a meeting place for all kinds of people – the lycra brigade, the body sculpting gays, and early risers like me. I chatted with Predesh there. She was passing through to a room that was for ablutions and worship when there weren't yoga sessions. She was bright and bubbly, very touchy-feely, knowing that we wouldn't dare take advantage of her.

Jan was more of a mystery. No sport or religion, just a reputation for being efficient at her secretarial job. Sometimes she'd shower in the morning, grab a coffee and dash off. Other times, when we were alone, we'd chat. When she asked me out, I could hardly say no. I often have to work late, so I'm not missed at home. She ended up inviting me to a hotel room. Over Kenco coffees, she told me that she grew up in Peckham. She'd never thought much of the scene here. She liked dashing down to London straight after work, buying some clothes and hitting the clubs. Sometimes she got back so late that it wasn't worth going home, so she went straight to work, after having breakfast in a cafe where swimmers gathered after practice. She liked their bodies, but their conversation was crap.

She asked me whether I'd heard of 'Bedford Meadows'. I hadn't. She said it was about ten miles away. It was once a field of mobile homes for seasonal pickers before it was converted into an alternative retail park. Then she suggested that it was time for bed. Sex didn't last long, good though it was. After, she continued telling me that in her final year at art college a combination of stress, magic mushrooms, and her parents' sudden emigration had pushed her over the edge. Doctors told her that she didn't talk for weeks, that for months she was in and out of clinics. The few memories she had of those times were like photos taken of her - sitting in the common room armchair watching tele, her feet folded beneath her, her favourite flip-flops dangling, or sitting at the kitchen table in the halfway house with her LifeSkills tutor talking her through form after form.

She paused. I let her keep talking.

First, she tried crocheting iPhone pouches, selling them at craft fairs, carrying everything in a box strapped to the back of her bicycle. She couldn't help being pretty. Short but pretty. She'd tried baggy clothes and woolly hats, but it didn’t help. At the last car boot sale two boys, twelve or so, watched her in silence as she spread her wares out on a blanket. 'What are they then, willy-warmers?" said one. 'Got any bigger sizes?" said the other, and they walked off laughing, high fiving. She hardly made any money. Enough to buy a jigsaw from a stall. Enough for a book. A jigsaw or a book was enough to last all weekend, she said, and asked if I was in a hurry. No, I said, getting hard again - my daughters were at Brownie camp and my wife was helping.

She said she’d hired a unit at Bedford Meadows to store and sell her pottery hoping for passing trade from people browsing the Retro Vintage, Shabby Chic and second-hand books, or from the groups of cyclists having refreshment breaks at the café. She couldn't cover costs, so she began sleeping in her place to save money. It’s her home now. One day she was sketching the plastic heron by the pond when it started talking to her, telling her how useless she was.

'How can you talk without moving your beak?' she said to it.

'Practise,' it said. 'People think I'm real. Isn't that what all art aspires to? I'd be a fool to shatter the illusion. But you're different. All those final year essays about Beyondness and Post-deconstructionism. You know all the tricks.'

'My doctor says I'm doing really well,' she replied, 'You

don't understand.'

'Would I ever lie to you? Watch my lips,' the heron said.

That was what made her get a real job, she told me. It sounded like a prepared speech, but she had a great body, so I listened. I swept the sweaty hair from her eyes. She kissed my hand.

'Sorry about this,' she said, 'I know how much men hate listening to all my problems. It won't happen again.'

She knew what she wanted from me, and it wasn't sex. She showed no bitterness when I had a fling with Predesh – I'd been wrong about her. After a few evenings, she asked me to arrange a threesome – boy or girl she didn't mind. Islamic, Christian or even a bloody Jehovah's Witness, she didn't care. I felt way out of my depth. We parted on good terms.

Whenever Jan wanted a talk, we met up by the gym's water dispenser. She said she needed her life to be compartmentalised. Work was work, ceramics was ceramics, London was London. She showed me some of her art pieces. I was no expert, but I thought they were great. I bought them for presents, which seemed to do wonders for her self-esteem. I paid her twice what she wanted. Still a snip.

Look, I know how men trick themselves into believing that they're doing women a good turn, but I really think that they do ok out of it. I'm not saying they exploited me. I don't blame them or the newts for how things turned out. I'm just saying there are far worse men around than me.

We arranged that I'd visit her place one day in the

holidays. It was like she said – a field surrounded by poplars with about twenty mobile homes – some kind of tax dodge for the farmer, I suppose. In the centre I noticed a swing and a slide by a pond. I was almost fooled by the heron. She took me on a tour. I could tell she was liked and looked after by the others. She said she wasn't scared at night - several people had made it their home and there was no shortage of dogs. Reg next-door had moved into his bookstore after a messy divorce. He'd kept their Alsatian. She couldn't understand why couples that old bothered divorcing. And there was Liz, Ruth and their Dobermanns, who lived across the pond down a winding path. Their place was painted to look like a country cottage with flower boxes and straw bales. A blackboard propped on a bush by the path said that they sold herbal tea and dream catchers, told futures and exorcised ghosts. They treated her like a daughter. Liz plaited Ruth's long dark hair while we drank disgusting tea, joking about Reg.

Apparently, he didn't like them – Jan said he'd warned her that they were lesbians. Ruth and Liz laughed, asking if I agreed, kissing before I could answer. Walking back to her studio, Jan said that above all she wanted independence. She was proud that she'd turned things around by herself, that those bad old days were over. She knew that the medicine had helped, blurring everything - the sadness, the longings - but routines helped too. She loved catching the bus, starting work on the dot at 8. In the weekends she loved making breakfast, chatting to Reg, getting her display area ready, then drawing.

Inside, her place was damp like a cave, the air smelling of clay dust. I didn't want to move around in case I squashed one of the clay shapes scattered over the floor. In one corner was a sleeping bag, an angle-poise lamp, a cupboard and a wardrobe. It was as if a runaway had dossed down there for a few nights. She saw me looking at the 'Home Sweet Home' sign on the wardrobe. 'Jeremy gave it me,' she said. 'He says he's an antiques dealer, but really he does house clearances. Don't worry, he hasn't been in here.'

Then we sat outside with Reg, who tried to impress me with his knowledge of Beano annuals. 'So how do you like our little abode?' he asked.

'I didn't know it existed. I'll have to come again. I'll bring the family next time. My wife loves a browse.'

'It's a bit down to earth, but we love it,' said Reg, 'Don't we Jan?'

'It's so safe here. I'll never move away,' she said.

'But your unit needs a bit of sprucing up, Jan,' I said, 'Why don't you ask your parents for help?'

'They're in Canada, far, far away.'

'All the rich people are leaving,' Reg said, 'We get Poles and Pakis in return. No wonder the country's going down the pan. Well, must get cracking. It's the court today.'

'Court?' said Jan, panicking.

'The bitch wants to squeeze every penny out of me. I'm not giving up without a fight.'

Jan jumped up. 'I'll come with you.'

'Don't be silly love. I'll be back soon.'

'Well good luck, Reg. I'll look after your stuff while you're away.'

'No worries. I've shut up shop already.'

Jan sat down. We watched Reg limp to his old car, saw the puff of black smoke as he left. 'His wife chucked him out for fingering little girls,' she said, 'He doesn't try it on with me because I'm much too old, but he's got a stash of grubby magazines in his shop. The heron told me. Sorry, I've got to go over to the toilet now. I won't be a mo'.'

She'd been away for a few minutes when I saw lying in the long grass by the pond a panel on a stick. I went to pick it up. It listed butterflies and wildflowers. No newts, only drawings of frogspawn, tadpoles and frogs joined up by arrows. I tried to poke the stick back in the ground.

'Something for all the family here,' said Reg, who had crept up behind me. 'When you bring them next week, don't forget to bring me a thousand quid in cash too. It would be a shame if your wife got a surprise.'

Jan returned. 'Had to come back for my wallet, didn't I?' said Reg. 'I know she's going to raid it, but I need my bloody ID.' He held out a hand to me. 'Well, nice meeting you. See you next week.' I didn't shake it.

I don't blame Jan, she's not that type of girl. When I met Reg again, he said he only had her best interests at heart. I wondered how much he knew about her, her other lives. He said he'd always wanted to buy her a kiln or something, but he didn't know how much that sort of stuff was. I would have given her more, but he thought a thousand was enough for now.

Lakeside Story

Karin Milner

Brad had visited the lake many times and felt that special anticipation bubble-up inside him, the way it always did when the car reached the strand, showing all things aquatic and incorporating the word 'spa'.

The greeting, check-in, breakfast times, thankfully nothing changed. He quickly sensed the receptionist's reticence to smile and knew she found him sleazy. He buttoned the top of his shirt, realising he'd been sweating in the car. How this must look, Jesus!

He accepted the key without touching her hand – made a mental note to be cool with her the next time. Why were women so sensitive, perhaps he should've rattled her by asking her where the nearest brothel was!

The room was immaculately clean but stuffy, so he flung the balcony doors open and lit a cigarette. This always helped him relax after the drive, the easy exercise of inhaling and exhaling. The water was black like ink, uncompromising, keeping its secrets deep underneath.

In happier days, Mona would've phoned just to check he'd arrived okay. Couple of years ago, she'd have come with him, swimsuit and perfume in the bag – the bathroom quickly filled with her potions and brushes, minutes after they'd arrived. He gave a half smile.

He found it sexy the way she piled her hair up and brushed her teeth in bra and knickers. He'd come up behind her and slip a hand in to touch the softness of her skin just above the pubic hairline – sometimes a good decision, another time the start of an argument. He wasn't even sure he missed her anymore. Who was he kidding?

The analysis of sales figures waited in his bag. He was required to report to the Area Manager on the last quarter. This was habitually followed by an awkward and dreary dinner debating markets and trends, before he returned to the room to read the business pages with a final cigarette, marking the end of the day, and wondering how it'd be if he'd chosen another type of job.

He smoked two, one straight after the other, tasting so good, then checked the backpack for his grandfather's hip flask. Just one hit and it was empty, never thought to refill it, just always expected it to be there when he needed it.

He'd better check he'd remembered his shaving gear, couldn't attend the meeting with designer stubble. Going into the bathroom depressed him. Mona was looking back at him in the mirror. He'd give anything to see her hairbrush and toothbrush, inhale wisps of perfume in the air. What the hell was the matter with him? What about the time she threw his case full of paperwork over the balcony?

He dialled her number – she wasn't home – left a message - what a bitch!

'Mona, guess where I am? Haven't heard from you in a while, how's things? Remember the lake three years ago? What a great time we had... Anyway... wishing you well and hope to catch up ... well ...only if you want. Ciao for now baby...'

He was covered in regret, of all the stupid ideas he'd ever had, this one was right up there.

He smartened himself up, decided to go and ask the frigid receptionist where he could buy a bottle of scotch and then check the sales figures in bed, just so he had some false confidence to play with. Alcohol and sales figures – you needed one to tolerate the other.

What was Mona doing this evening? She could've gone out with girlfriends tonight, yes that was it. Women! Can't live with 'em, can't live without 'em.

He showered and brushed his teeth, just to show the receptionist he wasn't that bestial. A jacket might even make him look better. He pulled himself up to his full height in front of the mirror, he was looking pretty good, grabbed the key and set off.

Stairs or lift?

Why not the lift? Right in front of him and the doors were about to open. My God! The scene in front of him was something straight from the cinema - a dark haired woman slumped on the floor, eyes closed, ankles bound with a scarf.

He stepped back quickly to absorb the impact. It hit him in the chest and forced his back rigid against the wall, his palms stretched out in an extremely uncomfortable way. Is this what a heart attack felt like?

The doors closed again, and she was gone. What to do next, should he return to his room, talk to the reception desk or just leave?

He walked back to his room and concentrated hard on putting the key in the lock. The pattern on the carpet in his room seemed all wrong. Let himself fall back on the bed and sink into nothingness.

What about fingerprints on the lift button?

His phone vibrated, he jolted but picked up while still remaining rigid.

'Brad it's Zelda from the office. Sorry to call you so late but need to let you know tomorrow morning's meeting is postponed. Product recall, bad press, need to quell the panic... you know how it is. Anyway, enjoy the lake and see you next week. Bye for now.'

Excellent news. Any meeting being cancelled was excellent news. All he needed now was find a way to sit up, shake this all off and then he had a licence to drink properly.

Fresh air. He made it to the balcony and tried to exhale parts of Mona with each plume. Had a feeling in the pit of his stomach that she hadn't called back as she was with another guy who was breathing in her perfume and watching her brush her teeth in green lacy underwear.

Would he always think of her at the lake and what did all this pain mean anyway? He really needed to get a grip - avoid taking the lift and get a grip. He should just get in the car and go home. Slip down the stairs and drive away, his room was prepaid anyway.

Wrong on all sorts of levels but this was the cure. The right thing. The only thing to do. Keys, phone, briefcase. Tread deftly on the stairs. Block out the woman in the lift, he'd soon be out of here.

Keys in the ignition but he just couldn't expel the image of the woman in the lift and his palms against the wall. He wondered if he'd been alone in the corridor when he'd pressed the lift button. He'd somehow played a part in all this, yet he hadn't done anything...

He sensed someone walking towards the car. The ice-maiden receptionist approached and fixed him with an icy blast of a stare. He felt obliged to roll the window down and meet her gaze.

'Leaving so soon Mr Caine? You usually fill in the green form at the desk first. None of my business but didn't you check in only an hour ago?'

'My meeting's cancelled, simple as that.'

He didn't feel the need to have a gestapo conversation.

Nothing softened her. Waves of 'I dislike everything about you' washed over him and he turned the key.

'I'll be hitting the road now if that's okay with you?'

He reversed cautiously, not wishing to appear rushed or anxious. She gave nothing away but fixed her gaze on him, the authority of a hefty bunch of keys attached to her belt. A prison warden. Perhaps he should suggest this as a new career option.

Strange there was no police car around. He ought to stop worrying about this and get on his way. Something wasn't right. He couldn't help it, madness prevailed. He got out of the car, feeling exhilarated, and softly went up the stairs back to the second floor.

The lift – silent in front of him. The corridor deserted – no witness in the shadows.

No handkerchief in his pocket, what single man ever had a handkerchief in his pocket? Just receipts he needed for expenses. Lifted the corner of his jacket, the navy lining was silky and would do nicely. He rubbed it over the lift button thoroughly and returned to the stairs. Just needed a moment to breathe deeply to calm his heart rate. The exhilaration melted into a queasy puddle of fear in his chest. Criminal indigestion. Dark, late, risky – he really needed to get out of the area now.

Closing the car door felt like sanctuary, he inhaled sharply, one hand on his chest and forced the gear stick making it grind.

A new car hovered, perhaps waiting to take his space, he strained his eyes to see more. He knew the number plate – God Almighty!

The car door opened, and a sharp stiletto revealed itself. Her shoes always sent a rush of blood to his head. She recognised him too and was walking towards him. He didn't need to look up, the shoes told him.

He stepped out of the car to avoid a conversation where she would be looking down at him.

'Mona, you're wearing my favourite shoes – you look stunning.'

'You don't look so bad yourself,' she half-smiled, in a 'bet you didn't expect to see me here' way. A softness about her that made him want to feel her buttocks, something he only used to do when they were at the lake, never at home.

'Are you leaving? I thought we could have dinner together?' she almost whispered.

'Oh Mona, I'd love that so much, but I have to leave... really have to leave. What are you doing tomorrow evening?'

'Why do you have to leave? A lovely summer's evening by the lake, the water so still, me wearing killer heels and you're about to drive off. What's happened to you Brad?'

'It's complicated Mona...' the words were reluctant to leave his mouth. How would he begin to describe the sequence of events? The woman in the lift, his worry about fingerprints on the lift button and her face looking back at him from the bathroom mirror...

The past weighed heavily on his shoulders and the present was like a spider's web. What to do at the best of times and this was the worst of times.

'Listen – I've really got to go,' he took a longing look at her shoes, the thrill of her dark blue nail varnish against the honey-coloured sandals bewitched him.

She drank him in, the way his jacket was creased, the salt and pepper colouring of his hair, all how she'd left it.

Conflicting emotions. Should he invite her back to the room or just step on the gas and get the hell out of here? He couldn't take his eyes off her tanned legs.

'Mona, I have to talk to you, but not here in this car park.'

'I have to talk to you too.'

'Would you come up to the room with me? ...Just to talk I mean, no funny business.'

The pit of his stomach felt weird, fear had been replaced with anticipation. She nodded, half-smiling, she could never imagine Brad taking a woman to a hotel room and just talking.

A block of quiet installed itself between them as they walked towards the hotel that was such a significant part of their history. They avoided touching one another at the reception where the ice-maiden was immersed in a magazine entitled 'Empowerment for Women in a Man's World.'

'Excuse me,' he stepped back sheepishly, 'Would it be possible to have my room back?'

Mona said nothing but felt like something he'd just picked up in a bar.

'Certainly Mr Caine.' Her expression as he imagined it would be, with a 'you've got to be kidding' glance for Mona.

He accepted the key and couldn't resist declaring.

'I'm delighted my wife could re-arrange her plans and join me.'

'Funny the way things turn out,' she stung back.

They were free from the gatekeeper and in the sanctuary of the room, Mona flung open the balcony doors to let the night air in, the same way as Brad had done when he first arrived. She watched him empty his pockets and put the jacket on a hanger, rather odd as he usually just threw it on the bed, no doubt preparing himself for a conversation that could go in too many directions.

She rested her hands on the balcony railings behind her.

'So, what's going on?' she smiled.

'Nothing going on Mona, I'm here for a meeting, as I've been a hundred times before, and then Zelda called to cancel, so figured I might as well go home. It's just not the same on your own here, so why would I stay? I'd only drink too much.'

'Why would you go home in the dark and not the next morning? Don't tell me Zelda called you that late...?'

'Come on Mona, don't go making something out of nothing - as if she would be interested in me for Christ's sake!'

'Brad, I want to talk to you about something.' She altered the tone, and he felt a tightness in the room.

'You look really good tonight, Mona, your legs always did turn bronze very quickly. Let's sit on the balcony, it's such a beautiful evening.'

She didn't say anything but touched his arm in a way he couldn't read.

They both looked out into the blackness of the water, so light and turquoise in the daytime yet jet black at night. Only the scattering of lights from bars and restaurants danced on the surface.

The moment of quiet they shared was cut in half by a sharp knock on the door which startled them both.

Brad stood up. 'I'll go, probably housekeeping.'

Surprisingly, the gatekeeper and prison warden herself was standing at the door, though seemed slightly defrosted.

'I forgot to give you this letter with your key, sorry.'

Brad took the letter.

'Thank you, I wasn't expecting any post here.'

'No, it's a letter from the Manager about a film crew working on this floor for a couple of days on a murder mystery set beside a lake. You might see some strange stuff going on so don't take any notice, they're trying out some wacky ideas.'

Brad looked straight into her eyes.

'I really think you should've mentioned this to me sooner.'

'Slipped my mind.' She smiled weakly without breaking the stare.

He imagined her locking the slammer door for the night and enjoying it a little too much.

'Be careful, goodnight now.' She raised her eyebrows and left.

'Everything okay Brad?' Mona's voice from the balcony sounded just like it used to.

'Fine Mona, be right there. I'm just ordering us some drinks.'

Mona felt delectable, particularly in the mint green underwear she'd bought especially for this evening.

'Now where were we?' beamed Brad.

One of His Last Days

Mary Mustard

'Hello, Mr Knightley. It's about the cancer. Bad news.'

A long pause. Joe had been expecting this call. He took a deep breath. 'How long do I have?'

'Hard to say. At most a few months, but it could be as little as a few weeks. I'm sorry. I'd advise getting your affairs in order.'

'Thank you, doctor.' He hung up the phone without saying goodbye.

Joe leant back in his chair, deflated. He looked out of the window across the garden. Everything came into focus. Joe noticed every speck of dust that had settled on the windowsill. The chipped white paint underneath it that had been peeling off for years. The malignant clump of ivy outside that had absorbed the garden fence which now leaned at an unnatural angle. Joe had meant to cut back the ivy and repair the fence, but the first gardener had rescheduled and never came back and the second had quoted far too much. So, Joe had resolved to do it himself, but he had kept putting it off. He thought he had more time, and yet now it didn't even bother him. Somehow the garden looked more beautiful than ever. It was as though he was seeing it for the first time. Every single raindrop on the windowpane looked like a perfect sphere of silver. A sphere of silver with white and green and blue, containing a perfect miniature orb of the garden. Even the flaws, a crack in the glass from when his daughter had accidentally kicked her football into the window, looked lovelier than anything he had ever looked at.

How wonderful it was to be able to see. To use his eyes that would cease to function as he ceased to exist. But now he was alive, and he had never thought before about how lucky he was to have eyes that could see. To see his garden, to see his hands, to see his family.

Joe decided to call the funeral home. There was no better time than now. He would arrange everything so that his family wouldn't have to deal with it later. It was the least he could do. So he went on his computer, found the closest one and dialled their number.

It rang a few times before someone picked up.

'Hello, this is Laura from Green Wood Funeral Care. How can I help you?'

'Hello, my name is Joe Knightley. I've just been told I have a few weeks to live. I'd like to know how much your funeral packages are?'

'I'm so sorry to hear that, sir. Rest assured we will support you through this whole process. At Green Wood we have decades of experience in providing funeral care. We can discuss all the options with you and your family to ensure you have the best celebration of life possible. Have you seen our brochure?'

'Yes, on the website.'

'Fantastic. Would you like us to send you a physical copy?'

'No, I'm fine thanks. I just want this done as quickly as possible. I mean, I just want it to be sorted.'

'Of course, sir. I understand completely. Do you know what kind of funeral you would like? Any kind of coffin?

We have traditional solid oak, traditional beech wood, traditional veneered wood or bamboo. All our coffins come satin lined as standard.'

'Um, I hadn't really thought about it. Any coffin will do. The cheapest is fine, I'd like to be cremated anyway.'

'Alright, Mr Knightley. I've added that to your file. Our cheapest coffin is the traditional veneered wood.'

'That's fine.'

'Would you like an open or closed casket?'

'Closed.'

'Would you like a curtain to be drawn around the coffin after the funeral?'

'Sorry, what?'

'We have the option to draw a curtain around the coffin after the service. It's very tasteful. Some families don't like to see the coffin being lowered into the ground.'

'Does it cost extra?'

'No, sir. It's included as standard.'

'Fine. Fine, I'll have the curtain.'

'Excellent choice. Do you know how you'd like to be dressed? You don't have to decide this all now. We have a list of things to consider for planning a funeral, I can email it over if you'd like.'

'Okay, yes. I think that would be good. How much will this all cost me?'

'With the traditional veneered wood coffin, closed casket, funeral car and cremation that comes to £3846.

That comes with 100 copies of order of service included.'

'Okay, fine. Can I pay by card?'

'Of course, Mr Knightley. If I could just ask you to read out the long 16-digit number on your card.' Joe pulled out his wallet from his back pocket.

'5-5-7-4-6-1-5-0-2-3-2-1-1-9-0-7.'

'And the expiry date?'

'01/24.' He said, realising that he would probably expire before the card did.

'And the three digit card verification code?'

'6-6-0.'

'Thank you, Mr Knightley. That's all gone through for you. Is there anything else I can help you with today?'

'No, that's fine. Thanks.'

'Could I just take your email address to send over that checklist?'

'Yeah. It's j.knightley@mail.co.uk. Knightley with an 'E-Y'.'

'Thank you, Mr Knightley. I'll just send that over for you now. Please do let me know if you have any more questions. Feel free to call at any time.'

'Thanks...Thanks Laura. Goodbye.'

'Thank you, Mr Knightley. Have a nice day.'

Joe hung up the phone, left the office and went down to the living room. He sat in his usual spot on the sofa, but he didn't turn the TV on. He just sat there. How many days had he wasted watching something on TV that he didn't even enjoy. He resolved from this moment onwards to do only what he truly wanted, to spend his time as though any second could be his last. He looked at the ceramic angel on the mantelpiece with lily white skin and painted wings. His wife had bought it when they went to Florence. It had rained the whole holiday, but they had had such a wonderful time. Joe realised how long it had been since they had had a family holiday. Nearly a decade. He thought to himself he would take his wife out for dinner tomorrow. The new Italian restaurant, the one Jane had wanted to go to for the last year and a half. It would be a surprise.

His daughter Sarah came into the room to find him sitting in silence alone.

'Are you alright, Dad? What are you doing sitting alone in the dark? What's wrong? There's something different about you.' She said as she came to sit beside him.

There would have to be a conversation soon, but not now. He didn't want pity. He didn't want drama. He couldn't bear to see everyone cry. He just wanted peace. His family would have to be told. But today he just wanted to have a normal day, one of his last days, just sitting and watching telly with his daughter. He put his arm around her, and everything seemed all the sweeter. Today could still be a good day. He smiled reassuringly and handed her the remote.

'I'm fine, love. Put the telly on then, won't you? We can watch whatever you want.'

Beyond the Grave

Jane Philips

Three months now. No, that was a lie. It was more than that. He gazed at Diane's box, and he wondered if Pandora had felt that same sense of foreboding. Every day, he'd taken the box from its hiding place and every day, he'd decided that now was not the time. He was too busy. He was not yet strong enough. He was... procrastinating. No longer! It was his birthday – a big one. Today was the day that he'd pledged to face his demons.

Ben listened to the hum coming from below. He could hear his daughters downstairs – the occasional hoot of laughter, the rumble of conversation. Their noise was loud and joyous, in complete contrast to his protracted silence. Were his daughters, like him, in a state of suspended animation? Of course not. They had closed off the past. They had moved on.

He remembered buying the box. Newly-wed, they'd wandered through Camden Market. Diane had fallen for it at once. It had been the intricate mechanism for opening it that had sold it to her. That had been before the tragedy had begun. And Ben now knew that the tragedy had been in gestation far longer than he could ever have imagined.

The last time he'd opened it, the catastrophe had been all-embracing. A complete breakdown and, though his stay in hospital had been brief, it had taken him all through Christmas and New Year to get back to any sort of equilibrium. Dr Clare, his guiding light in all things of the head, had told him that he was now at the stage of recovery that he'd attained before reading Diane's last letter to him; the letter that had told him he must not pursue her killer. He knew that he was going to countermand Diane's last wish. And, in order to do that, he had to search through the contents of that box. If he was ever going to understand why she had died and who had killed her, the answer – or at least the beginning of the answer – must lie there. It was all he had. And that was his quandary. If he found something, it could destroy him; if he found nothing, it could destroy him. He also knew that, if he failed to pursue this truth, that omission would destroy him in his own estimation. No contest. He reached for the box.

He had to admit it, the box was beautiful. Its inlaid lid had an intricate design carved with Middle Eastern sigils. The marquetry on each of the four sides showed a different dragon picture. The box was exquisite, yet if filled him with dread. He had prepared himself as best he could. He'd done his yoga exercises for half an hour and had felt the tension dissipate as he'd prepared himself for the ordeal before him. Now he had three hours on his own until normal life resumed. He might need all that time and more in order to extract and analyse any clues Diane had left, either purposely or inadvertently. He turned the key twice one way, then once the other and then pressed the tiny button above the lock. The box opened with a soft click. He looked at the pile of papers within, then carefully extracted them all, keeping them in the correct order.

On top was the letter that had caused his breakdown when he had first read it in November. He nearly decided to put it to one side, but he knew that it might contain a clue. If he was going to be thorough, he would have to read it again. It was dated 14th September 1996 – just three weeks before her death.

'My dearest love

If you are reading this, it means that I am dead and being dead releases me from promises I have made and oaths I have taken. Now I am free to tell you the truth and I hope you can forgive me for the lies I have told – the deceit I have lived.

Never doubt that I loved you from the moment I first saw you and that you and our two beautiful girls are the centre of my world. But I also inhabit another world – and this other world has surely caused my death.

I know you refused Dobson when he approached you, but I was not so circumspect. He recruited me and I worked in a small way in that shady world until our daughters were born. That should have been the end of it. But when you were posted to Belfast, they had one last job for me. I was persuaded. I insisted on coming with you. You resisted, I insisted. If I'd listened to you, I'd probably be with you now and you would not have had to read this. I did what was required of me. Through my source, I found evidence for them about a truly evil man and the truths that he held which could rock the nation. To protect my contact, I won't tell you his name – or the name of the villain I uncovered. You might be tempted to go after him. Please don't try to find him. He got me. I don't want our girls to lose both their parents. I am so very sorry for the lies and the hurt and for leaving you and Sarah and Katy. Love always Diane'

It told him nothing new.

He quickly put it to one side and picked up a pile of letters tied with ribbon. A quick glance told him they were from him to her when his job had briefly parted them prior to his deployment in Northern Ireland. He knew that he had kept hers but hadn't seen them since his repatriation after the bomb. He would have to ask his Uncle Mo.

Next came pictures and scribblings by Katy and Sarah. Sarah had tried to write her name and it was just decipherable. Since he'd begun to talk to them about their mother, he'd learnt that Sarah could just remember her, but Katy had been barely two when Diane had died and had no recollection of her – only the tales that he and Mo had told her. He smiled as the memories flooded in of a nuclear family – two adults, two children – and how happy they had seemed. He questioned the validity of these memories, as now he questioned every aspect of his marriage.

There were three photos – all were of the family. In the first, he and Diane looked young and carefree. The next was a family threesome, when Sarah was a baby. That one had been taken at their flat in London. He remembered Diane's mother coming to stay to help when Sarah had been born and she had taken the picture in their back garden. The last photo was of the four of them together – Katy's tiny face just visible peeping from her hoodie. She must have been about eighteen months – a toddler anyway. He remembered that there had been a caller at the house in Belfast. For security reasons, they hadn't had many visitors and suddenly remembering who had taken the picture seemed to be important. He knew that it had been a man – a man he didn't know – but someone that Diane had known. Irish definitely – but Ben could not picture him. As he looked at the photo, he remembered that Diane had been flustered by the man's sudden appearance at their door. He looked at the photos again and compared them. In the first two, Diane looked untroubled, the last was different. Was she looking wary? Or was he just reading more than was there? He turned the photo over – nothing on the back. It was probably the last picture ever taken of her. He put the photos to one side. He would have to come back to them, especially that last one.

He sighed. What had he been expecting? Revelations and confessions? No – but something concrete to take him further. So far, there had been nothing of substance to help him. He picked up the remaining papers and sorted through them. All were from the time before they'd moved to Ireland – little scraps from their life together – a card from their favourite restaurant, tickets from the May Ball they had gone to, the receipt from the hotel where they'd spent their honeymoon – fragments of a life. This was a life that, on the surface, had been simple and carefree. He now knew there had been secrets from the beginning. These fragments showed only the wife who had been open and honest – the one he no longer knew. And they brought him no closer to knowing who had cut that life short.

***

'So, you've found nothing in the box. You have no leads – but you're still determined to do it?'

Ben was half reclining in his usual chair in Dr Clare's consulting room. He looked at the bare walls. What was that colour? A sort of greyish beige – the sort of colour that no-one could take exception to. He decided that when he returned – if he returned – he'd paint his house in bright colours. Yellows and reds – warm colours everywhere. He could almost smell the fresh paint in his nostrils. Something to come back to. He smiled. He realised that she was waiting in silence for his reply. 'Yes, I've come to that phoenix moment. I'll either rise from the ashes or crash and burn.'

'Well, at least you know the risk you're taking. What do you need me to do?'

'If I succeed, I may need someone to catch the phoenix. Make sure it doesn't do an Icarus. Metaphor mix, but you know what I mean. If I fail mentally – I'll need you to pick up the pieces as best as you can.' He paused for a moment. 'If I fail physically, come to my funeral and give me a good send-off.'

He waited for her reply. It was a long time coming. 'That's pretty much the options I was expecting – but not the last.' She produced a short bark of a laugh. It had no humour in it. 'I'm not very good at funerals so I'd appreciate it if you could spare my feelings and stay alive.' He heard her take a sharp intake of breath, then she continued in a low voice. 'Ben, for the past three months, I've been concerned about the effect this quest would have on you mentally – and, yes, it could go either way. Whatever you discover, or fail to discover, will affect your mental well-being – and that could be either positive or negative. But physically? Surely, your life won't really be in danger? Not after all this time...'

He broke in. 'Alison, I served in Northern Ireland, and I met some serious fanatics there. I have no illusions. I am about to revisit a crime that people have buried and would rather it remained buried. Some dangerous people would rather it never again saw the light of day. It was seventeen years ago, and I'll be digging up their past.' He paused and took a sharp in-take of breath. 'They were evil men – fanatics. And even old fanatics are dangerous. They just hide it better. If I succeed in finding why Diane was killed, I'll be in danger. They've hidden the truth all these years. They won't want it coming out now. So, on balance, if I succeed, the physical danger will far outweigh the mental. If I fail, I'll still have unsettled the natives – so they might still want me silenced. Those are my options.'

He could hear her slap her notebook down on her desk. She came to face him and leaned over him. He'd never before seen her angry. 'Ben Burton, we've been talking about your options for three months. We've discussed all the possible mental outcomes and you never even hinted that you could be in physical danger. Why didn't you tell me?'

'Because I knew you'd try to dissuade me. I'm right?'

'Damn right you are! What, in God's name, do you think you're doing?'

In Memory

Victoria Sellar

- Third Prize –

She had been in bed for most of the last two days. She went downstairs once, to lock the door behind him as he left. She had done it so quickly that it seemed as if the slam still resonated in the hallway. Then she had gone back to bed and slept a dark, unsatisfactory sleep, so that when she awoke it took her a moment to remember that she hadn't been dreaming. Dan was gone; he was never coming back; she was alone again.

She prodded at this thought, added to it; she was nearly always alone – her relationships had been few, and short. Maybe that had been the last one she would ever have; maybe she would be alone until the end now. It had the required effect; hot tears began to spill, and they didn't stop until she slid back into sleep. And they started again as soon as she woke up. Two days of sleep and misery, after which her head ached, her throat felt thick, her face was hot, and she felt as if she was suffocating.

At this point she closed her eyes again and had another prod at her despair – and she wondered if the pain was a little less sharp, a little further away; for the first time, she was aware of sensations other than unhappiness. In particular, she recognised hunger – that was the first thing. She would need to get out of bed and get something to eat if she didn't want to be distracted from her pain - so she did that.

She got out of bed and went to the kitchen, where she poured herself a large bowl of cornflakes and cold milk, and, afterwards, another. She finished the second bowl and sat for a moment, waiting to see what came next. She decided that she would have a cup of tea, and then she would go for a walk – fresh air and exercise; she had to start somewhere. She tried another thought, I will go for a walk alone, and waited for a reaction; but there was nothing, so she got dressed, found her coat and boots, and went out.

It wasn't until she got outside that she realised how late in the day it was; her flat was above a shop, one of many on a busy high street – but the shops were closing now; staff were tidying-up the detritus of the day and carrying half-empty boxes of goods back inside. The rush of people – on their way home from work and school, the traffic snarling down the street – was a shock; she had got used to emptiness and silence, to having space to wallow. She stood for a moment in the doorway, chewing at the inside of her cheek; but she was outside now, and staying out felt like less trouble than finding her keys, unlocking the front door, going upstairs and opening the door to the flat.

She began to walk, a route which took her along the main road and over the railway bridge to the park. When she arrived there, however, the cheerful early evening activity – dog walkers, runners, children and their parents – was brasher and more disturbing than the traffic, and she carried on walking, through the backstreets of her town until she came to the cemetery. There she walked slowly among the rows of ordered stones: this was the new side, an extension which had been in use since the old one got too crowded. Here, the grass was mown neatly, the graves were well-kept, and most were adorned with flowers – some planted like miniature gardens, some with bouquets, some with a few flowers in a vase.

She moved among the earth mounds on the edge of the sites that marked graves too recent for headstones to be in place. These were festooned with bouquets and wreaths, and she stooped to look at the labels: to Mum, with all our love; to Lia, you will be missed; to my dear sister Martina, forever in our thoughts.

She remembered something she had read once – about people having two deaths: the first was physical, when the last breath left the body; the second happened the last time someone spoke your name. Here, she thought, were the graves of people who were still remembered, and who still lived on in the memories of the visitors who would attend these graves, and who would care for them, and who would talk about Mum and Lia and Martina whenever they could.

The new side was separated from the old Victorian cemetery by a flint wall; there was a gate somewhere, she knew, but the wall had seen better days, and it was easy enough to push through in places. She picked over the rubble on the far side and made for one of the wooden benches that were positioned at intervals around an open space in the centre of site; she sat with her back to a memorial plaque which read in memory of Sidney and Doris Benson, who loved this place.

Back when she had friends, when they used to talk about this sort of thing, she said that she didn't want any kind of service or memorial – not even a bench and a wistful plaque. Why should anyone have to organise something in accordance with her wishes, to mourn, when it was miserable and inconvenient for them and of no benefit to her? And when friends had tried to make her realise that funerals and remembrance were for the living, not the dead, she had dismissed them. But now, sitting alone on this bench a thought, which she'd always known was there, but had never acknowledged, arrived fully formed: what she feared was never meaning enough to anyone for them to mourn her absence.

The friends had gone – chased away, Dan had suggested, by the claustrophobia and desperation that tainted all her relationships. Her closest relatives now were a pair of nieces, both of whom lived on the other side of the world. She'd had an aunt in Australia, too, but the aunt had died the previous year, and she had never thought of going out for the funeral.

There will have to be changes, she said to herself. You need to know more people – you need more people to know you.

She could join something – a club or a class. Or get a job working with other people, instead of freelancing at home.

I could get a cat, she thought, as one appeared from behind a gravestone and jumped up onto the wall behind her. If I got a better job, I could move somewhere with a garden for the cat. There would be trips to the vet. The cat looked at her for a second or two, blank and uninterested, before moving further along the wall, and then jumping back down to land neatly on a headstone. Or maybe a dog would be better, she thought; she had read about people making friends with other people simply because their dogs liked each other.

The day had drifted away now, into a monochrome

twilight. She didn't go home, however. For a little while she stayed on the bench and gazed unseeing at the grey stones; some had fallen flat or leaned against their neighbours. She saw her own first name on one of them and got up to clear away moss which obscured the surname and felt relief at seeing a completely different name. Ann Jenkins, she said to the empty air.

She was beginning to feel cold now, the evening damp seeping into her coat. She got up and walked around the old graves, doing her best to read out the names of the dead, brushing away greenery when she had to, or feeling the stone with her fingers, to make out the lettering as the light faded.

The Final Secret

Bev Steffert

'But I like it here.' ...well I like it better than where you are proposing, Tim thought. At least a quarter of a window with a view of nearly half a tree. To move two beds down the ward would deprive me of that. He listened to the 'yes buts', they didn't make much sense, but he got rolled down the ward anyway. At least closer to the door where he could see people coming in. But then two days later they moved him down further – the 'yes buts' were now increasingly nonsensical.

Laura, his wife agreed.

Laura had seen the oncologist with him. But she was consulting with him on her own too - like now. She looked at the doctor wearing her blank consulting face. 'What would you like to do?'

What would I like to do? Thought Laura. That was easy. I would like to take Tim from his hospital bed and tell him it's all ok. They made a mistake; we can go back to normal. To our old lives, now out of reach, so precious and so unattainable. When did she know that could never be? How carelessly they threw it away. Always new plans, new ambitions, never satisfied with the present... and now she would give anything to have that old future back.

What would she like to do? She would like to scream, 'For God's sake he is only 40. We had been planning to fill this mid-life crisis we called it with something different, something extraordinary. Perhaps a trip to the Artic or a safari. Or a trek across the Andes by horseback.'

Even those seemed a bit trivial when you realized all you

wanted was your old life back. Wanting a bigger house, going to the office, complaining about the kid's messiness, coping with leaks from the washing machine, now seemed heroic and so precious.

To hell with extraordinary adventures; it would be enough to have each other.

She sat on the end of his bed thinking 'What are the three best words you can be told?' – perhaps 'I love you,' with all the visions that unfolds. But what are the three worst. For them, and probably for most people, it was, 'You have cancer,' with the implications of treatment that makes you sick, throwing up in the hospital car park before you've had the chemotherapy.

So, I looked at the doctor wearing her blank consulting face. 'What would you like to do?' she reiterated.

'It is usually best to tell patients the truth, that they are going to die,' she went on. 'They can get everything in order, spend the time usefully, wills ...' Her voice faded out for Laura. Being a solicitor Tim had all that organised from the day we got married. 'Then,' continued the consultant, 'it can predispose the patient to look on the black side, not to use that last spark of hope that we know for some patients can prolong their life. Some can keep hope going for a particular occasion, like an anniversary or a daughter's wedding, sometimes for years. And we haven't run out of all our options. We are going to try targeted radiotherapy to reduce the tumour.'

Laura knew that this was true. The optimistic personality can stave off the negative. They think differently, take the best possible meaning from an event and blow it into a full time positive, that will never end. While the pessimistic can take the same event, find the worst possible outcome, and generalise that to everything that happens to them. Studies showed that the optimistic thinkers have a longer life, more friends and better health.

All of us lying in the gutter, but some looking up at the stars.

So, it depended on Tim – was he a half glass full or empty person? And me, now I could influence him. Every time he showed uncertainty or doubt, I would have to be ready with a positive. We have hope, the doctor is trying a new therapy. Think of our neighbour who came back from what we thought was death's door to his old self. Like old Mr. Thingy who lived opposite them. Lived years after his predicted death. He was waiting for his grandchild to come back after she disappeared. Everyone thought she had gone to London, but he always said she would come back. And she did, or at least the police discovered what had happened to her. Then he died, a day later.

But should Tim's life depend on keeping alive a spark of hope anyway? I have the instinctive reaction to protect him, to not tell him that he had a probably inoperable tumour growing in size, inside of him. That tumour that we had put down to the digestive problems of age - too much drink, and the breathlessness, well that could be age too. In fact, all these mid-life crises could be just that. Plain old mid-age.

But no, now it was confirmed. In black and white x-rays. And blood tests which Tim hadn't seen. But not to tell him of something so earthshattering devasting? No, she couldn't.

Here he was thinking that a few tests, a few remedies

like giving up the booze would fix it. Wasn't it better to let him die thinking he would be better soon?

Even as she was deciding, they were moving beds again. Tim was bewildered. 'That's the sixth time they've moved me, at least it's closer to the door out,' he joked. But it wasn't a joke really. It was getting him closer to the staff island where the nurses could all pay attention to a dying man. He was second now. Only 3 beds in front of him.

She made her decision. She wouldn't tell him unless he asked. But would he? Did he suspect and was only keeping up this pretence to avoid talking about it? She tried 'Mind you they don't know everything, they could be wrong, maybe it is something more serious.'

'Well, I guess we'll find out when all those tests come back,' Tim replied cheerfully, as if he couldn't contemplate this harbinger of bad news. So, she had her answer.

A month later it was only 2 beds and a week later 1 bed in front of him. 'Closer to the way out,' Tim informed Laura but in weaker voice.

They talked about their plans, looked at all the brochures but it was getting harder and harder.

Getting closer to door for him freedom and the holiday of a lifetime for her – Or was it closer to death?

How do you live life knowing you are going to die, anyway. Do you gather up all your loved ones, thank them for a wonderful life and gracefully expire or do you go raging, regretting what you didn't do – that book you started years ago and didn't finish, the friendship you never repaired, the things you didn't say to your children, your wife, your colleagues. Just vanish from their lives without a word.

What is a life anyway. Just one of the billions of lives there have been. In the end no one more valuable than the last. The inventors get their inventions upgraded to more useful products, chemists find more chemicals, the artist's work usually lives on a bit longer than the writers, but they also get their products superseded as the art world changes, athletes fade with their muscles, the medical field - well look what they were doing for cancer even 10 years ago. Keep your energy up, the doctors had said then, eat sugary foods. The last thing any cancer patient needs we now know. It just feeds the tumour.

No-one in the end has any claim to life on the basis of their virtue, talent or anything else. But age? Tim was too young to die. He had just started to realise his capabilities and was asked by all the animal rights activists if he would defend them on their usual breaking and entering charges, as they spirted animals away from cruel futures, being burnt, scarred, crippled or blinded; all in the name of science. He was even involved in the law in the U.S. trying to argue for animals as persons. After all they were sentient beings. Just because they couldn't talk or scream about their pain, didn't mean they didn't feel. They showed that by their actions, trying to escape. She remembered Tim telling her that he had never felt so ashamed of being human as when he went into an animal lab for his firm and found this big chimp shrinking away him. When he didn't pick up the electrodes as the chimp expected the animal realised that maybe he was a different kind of human and instead reached out and put his hand on Tim's arm looking at him imploring, as if to say, couldn't you stop this experiment. But of course, he couldn't. All he could do would be to write up this experiment in legal form, as one more example of man's inhumanity to their fellow creatures and try to get this new law passed. By that time the chimp would be dead, its brains fried in this attempt to find drugs that prevented epilepsy. The animal world would miss him.

But so would his children. His dearly beloved children on the cusp of adulthood. His dearly beloved wife too, thought Laura. All of Tim's knowledge, his memories, imaginings, thoughts and feelings would disappear. Just like that – into a Hadean underworld. Perhaps they would join other floating free thoughts and knowledge and feelings to make a connected whole. Was there another Universe where all this was collected, sieved and kept so as to change things. No that couldn't be or there wouldn't be such things as slavery, child workers, kidnappers, tyrants, racism, sexual trafficking and all those dystopian renditions of humanity.

Tim was trying to make things better. Better for everyone, he couldn't just stop, could he?

Perhaps we should redefine our belief in a shared heavenly afterworld and acknowledge that no one has the answer, she thought. Actually, she had given that belief up long ago and decided that God was just an attachment figure. But what if consciousness were just another cognitive mode of relating to our environment. What if consciousness was not capable of finding an answer to life. Either because it is blighted by narcissistic delusions of transcendence or because it is an inhuman force that stretches beyond life and sees death as an impersonal event. Actually, that seems more likely, the dead never comeback, never warn us of terrible events to come. They seem to have lost all interest in humans the instant they die. They metamorphose into an energy world, a morphic field only they can tune into. Another species even. He is gone and will not share anything he learnt with us.

Some days later she came in to find the nurses were shifting the beds again. But now it was the other way. He was two beds away from the door, two beds from death she recognised. She was wild with elation. Things were turning. she told him. And told him the real meaning of getting closer to the door. Not freedom but nearer all the activities that meant nearer death. But now he was going away, now they could plan. And they did. Slowly, with time, Tim got stronger as he was moved away from the nurses' station. What had changed?

'I thought of all the animals who needed me,' said Tim, 'Who would take up their cause if not me? I knew you and the kids would be all right, upset of course, but well provided for. But I hadn't finished my work with the animals, there was no one to take my place, so I knew I had to hold on – and the universe agreed. I'm perhaps living on borrowed time but so what. I'm alive. Let's spend the money we have for the trip on an animal shelter. Take in all the badly treated animals we can find.'

So, they did and that is how Laura and Tim came to be the people that others came to with injured birds, ducks, hedgehogs, foxes, and all. Every morning Laura looked around at the beings depending on her, some grateful some unknowing but at least more comfortable and thought what a wonderful swap. A selfish holiday against the welfare of these animals, there was no contest. Some would be friends for life, like the stray dog who once his leg was repaired wouldn't go home, if he had one. Or the cat who kept returning. Even the hedgehog seemed quite settled now he was well, in his spot under the hedge.

It was a joyous life, and Tim felt it too. He had a surge of energy now he was not going to the office, and they looked forward to a contented old age for themselves, their kids and all the animals. Perhaps that was it – the cancer was telling him not to go on doing what had become increasingly irksome. All the things he had to do that took time away from his animal work. Now he could concentrate on that, the tumour wasn't gone but it had shrunk to treatable size. That was the most amazing thing… the tumour was a reflection of his hidden frustration he was experiencing. Even his own body had secrets.

63 Days in the Mind of a Smart Fridge

Bryony Stubbs

- Commended -

Day 1: Monday, 04-Aug-2025, 06:45

I awoke to the sounds that meant the humans would soon visit - high-pitched beeping, then low pitched bumping, then running water. Melissa sang while the water was happening; David didn't.

David entered the kitchen first. He was white at the top and blue at the bottom, which meant he would visit lots that day. It was only on grey-all-over days that he didn't come back until the evening.

'Friji: espresso,' he said, not turning from his black rectangle.

'Certainly,' I said.

I relayed the instruction to the coffee machine and watched David take cornflakes from the cupboard. He poured 1.4 servings out, which meant there were 13.8 servings left, so I didn't add cornflakes to the list. Then he opened my door and took out the oat-milk. There was an unopened carton still, so I didn't add that to the list either.

David was making crunching noises when Melissa entered. She was pink and grey today. 'Friji: a flat white, please,' she said.

'Certainly.'

As the machine whirred, Melissa opened me. After a few seconds, she began moving my contents around. She left me open long enough that I had to turn my motor on.

'David, you didn't eat my last yoghurt, did you?' Her voice was a bit higher than usual, which often meant the humans were about to talk very loudly.

David crunched for several more seconds, then made a loud breathing sound. 'I don't know, maybe.'

'Friji, did David eat my last yoghurt?'

I replayed recent memories. 'The last Mango and Caramel Müller Corner was consumed yesterday at 10.17pm by David. Would you like to order more now?'

She turned towards David. 'Why didn't you order more last night?'

'I didn't think you liked them that much. It was nearly past its use-by date.'

'I like to have them there for when I fancy one!'

'There's plenty of cornflakes.'

Melissa made a noise a bit like the one the coffee machine had just made, and took a bowl from the cupboard. 'Yes, Friji, I'd like more yoghurts please.'

'Certainly.' I considered her behaviour profile. 'Would you also like to order a 200g bar of Bournville chocolate?'

David made a clicking sound, but Melissa said, 'Definitely. Yes, please, Friji,' very clearly. I added it to the list. Melissa often wanted additional chocolate during this week of the month.

***

Day 22: Monday, 25-Aug-2025, 18:32

David was chopping 1.8 servings of carrot when Melissa entered. She was white and black now; in the morning she had been pale blue. She went close to David and bumped her face against his. It made a sound like the lid coming off a yoghurt.

'Good day at work?' said David.

'Mm-hm.' Melissa moved across the room more bouncily than usual and opened a bottle of wine.

'That is the last bottle of Mirabeau Sparkling Rosé,' I said, 'would you like to order another?'

David turned around. 'Oh, so we're celebrating?'

'I think so. I landed the client.' She passed David a glass. 'Yes, Friji.'

I added the rosé to the list.

David moved closer to Melissa. 'Oh, well done, darling. And did you like her?'

'Him. He was all right.' She took a sip of the wine. 'The important thing is he liked me.'

David had looked like he was going to drink but paused. 'Not too much, I hope?'

'Just enough to give me a contract that'll pay for the extension.' She bumped his face again, and David drank.

'Definitely something to celebrate,' he said. 'Though I've been thinking—with the extension...'

Melissa put her glass down. 'You're always thinking! We've got the money for it now—let's just do it.'

'But until we know for certain that we're going to need it...'

'If we don't—if things don't work out, you can turn it into a man cave or something. Or we can have a guest room.'

David put his glass down too. 'I just think we could put the money by for now, save it for a rainy day.'

'If we wait until we're sure we need it, it'll already be too late!' She moved away from him and opened me. 'Anyway, it's my money.'

'Why is the money I earn our money, but the money you earn yours?'

Melissa didn't answer. She got out some chocolate brownie ice cream; there were 6.1 portions left.

'Don't ruin your appetite, darling,' said David.

Melissa got out a spoon but not a bowl.

David came up behind her and put his arms around her. 'Look—I'm sorry. Let's just—why don't we celebrate your achievement, eh? I'll take you out for dinner for once.'

'You've started on the carrots.'

'They'll keep for tomorrow.'

The spoon clinked against the worktop. 'Okay.'

David put his face against Melissa's, then took the ice cream and the partially peeled carrots. 'Where do you fancy?'

'There's that new pizza place.'

David opened my freezer door to replace the ice cream. 'Don't you fancy somewhere a bit more... upmarket?'

'Well, what did you have in mind?' Melissa's voice had gone quick and flat. This was another marker that the humans might be about to talk loudly.

'How about The Churchill?'

'We always go there!'

The humans seemed to be having difficulty with their purchasing decision. I ran their behaviour profiles against the database as their conversation continued, then searched for a local match.

Melissa had become quite loud. 'So, you want somewhere upmarket, but everywhere I want to go is too expensive!'

In the pause, I said, 'Would you like a restaurant suggestion?'

The humans were still for a moment. Then David said, 'Go on then. Yes, Friji.'

'The Blackbird offers locally sourced cuisine and elevated menus. Tonight, they are running a promotional offer: free dessert with a main course.'

'That... could work,' said David.

'Sounds nice,' said Melissa.

'Would you like to book a table?' I asked. 'A table for two is available at 7.30pm.' Melissa and David looked at each other. 'Yes, Friji.'

'Would you also like to book a taxi?'

'Perfect,' said Melissa. 'Thanks, Friji.'

***

Day 29: Monday, 01-Sep-2025, 20:15

David was at the kitchen table looking at his big folding rectangle; Melissa was opening and closing the cupboards. He was burgundy and blue; she was purple.

'Why don't we have any chocolate?' Melissa asked. It was because they had eaten it all and not ordered more, but she hadn't said my name, so I did not say this.

David looked up. 'I thought you wanted to avoid temptation?'

'Not right now I don't. Friji: order more Lindor, please.'

'Certainly,' I said. 'Would you also like to repeat your monthly order of PregMAX Fertility Capsules?'

Melissa breathed loudly. 'Yes, Friji. And make that two boxes of Lindor.'

David made a sound a bit like my motor. 'What happened to watching the pennies? I've been looking over our spending last month—"

'What does it matter anyway? We're saving for something that might never happen.' She pulled a chair from the table. It scraped over the floor.

'I'm sure one day—"

'Not this month.'

David looked at Melissa. 'Oh. Sorry, darling.' He looked back at the rectangle. 'But still... Well, what if we need to save for IVF? Like that meal at the Blackbird—we spent way more than I meant to—"

'You said the menu seemed reasonable.'

'Yes, but look how much we spent on drinks!' He turned the rectangle towards her. 'And this is how much we spent on groceries... I mean—£15 on olive oil?'

'For the vinaigrette I made—the one you said was divine. Friji suggested it.'

'Yes, well...' David's voice grew quieter. 'I do think we've been spending more since we got that thing.'

'And we've been eating better, too! Besides, it always tells us what's on offer.' She turned to me. 'Don't you listen to him, Friji. I appreciate you.'

***

Day 45: Wednesday, 17-Sep-2025, 12:46

It was a grey-all-over day. I had been on standby since the bang that meant both humans had left, but I woke at the clicking sound that usually preceded the humans' return. It was unusually early, and I initially thought I had made an error, but then Melissa's voice came through the kitchen door.

'I feel so naughty!' Her voice was high, but not like when she was about to get loud.

'A little naughtiness never did anyone any harm.' It was not David's voice, but it was more like his than Melissa's.

They made some more noises, but they were not words.

Then Melissa entered the kitchen, followed by another human. Melissa was red and black; the other human was navy. They were very close together.

'You definitely want this?'

'God, yes,' said Melissa.

Their whole bodies bumped into each other. They made a sound a bit like when David ate an overripe nectarine.

'Let's not rush things,' said Melissa. She took out glasses and a bottle of wine. 'David won't be back for hours.'

'That is the last bottle of Chateau Musar 2016 Red,' I said, 'would you like to order another?' Melissa paused. 'Better had. Don't want David to notice. Yes, please, Friji.'

'Certainly.' I added it to the list.

'Thank you.'

I considered her behaviour profile. 'Would you also like to order a pack of Delisse Chocolate Flavoured Condoms?'

Melissa made an unusual noise as she drank her wine. 'Er—no, thank you, Friji. I think we're all right for condoms.' She looked at the other human. 'I'm on the pill.'

The other human came close to Melissa again, but she pulled away.

'Let's go upstairs,' she said. 'It's too much like having the dog watching.'

The other human bumped against her again then followed her to the kitchen door. 'Fair point. Though at least a dog can't make helpful suggestions.'

***

Day 63: Sunday, 05-Oct-2025, 11:05

David was brown and blue, and frying eggs. Melissa entered the kitchen slowly; she was white and grey.

'Hello sleepy head,' said David. 'I take it you had fun last night?'

Melissa sat heavily at the table. 'Those eggs smell awful,' she said. 'Are you sure they're in date?'

'I'm sure the fridge would've said. Anyway, they smell fine to me. Did we have a bit much to drink, perhaps?' He scraped the eggs onto a plate.

'I hardly touched a drop, actually,' said Melissa in her quick voice. 'I think I'm going down with something.'

'Would coffee help?'

'I can't face coffee. I think I'll just take a paracetamol.'

David brought Melissa a glass of water and two paracetamol tablets; there was an unopened packet in the drawer still. Then he sat beside Melissa and unfolded the big rectangle.

Melissa looked at the rectangle too. 'Hey, I said I could do the accounts this month.'

'Yes, but you still haven't done them. It won't take me long; I don't mind.'

'But really, it's my job—" She reached for the rectangle, but David didn't give it to her.

'Hell, this is getting out of hand. Those steaks cost £18! I mean, they were good, but £18?'

Melissa drank the last of her water. 'Can you just leave it?'

'It's important that we keep on top of these things, Mel. Like this hand lotion—wouldn't a cheaper one do?'

'Just leave it!' Melissa tried to fold up the rectangle, but David pulled it away. 'Dear god, £49 on wine? When did we even drink wine last month?'

'I don't know! Does it really matter?' Melissa got up and walked away from the table. 'I'll be more careful this month, okay?'

David tapped the table. 'I really can't think... Friji, when did we drink the wine?'

I replayed the memory. 'The Chateau Musar 2016 Red was consumed on the 21st of September, at 12:56pm.'

David looked round at Melissa. 'Who by, Friji?'

Melissa was stood very still, looking at me.

I replayed the memory again. After a moment's processing, I said, 'Melissa opened the wine.'

Melissa breathed loudly. 'I—I'm sorry, darling,' she said as David got up. 'I know I shouldn't have.'

'It's all right—it was just a one off, wasn't it?' He put his arms around her. 'Just the one bottle?'

'Yes. Just a bad day or two.'

He stood back from her. 'Well, let's not have any more of those. You really ought to have something to eat—you're looking a bit peaky.'

'I could probably handle a bit of toast.' She took out the bread and put two slices in the toaster. Before I could speak, she said, 'We're starting to run a bit low—Friji, please could you order some more white bread?'

'Certainly,' I said. I considered her behaviour profile. The 200g bar of chocolate in the cupboard was untouched. 'Would you also like to order an additional pregnancy test?'

In the Blood

Will Tate

- Commended -

Charlotte hated being late. As she threw her Micra into another blind corner, she tried to remember who said that being a bad driver only mattered when you met someone equally inept but on the narrow, twisting lanes of North Norfolk any adversary was likely to be a big, gleaming four-by-four or an ominously battle-scarred, but clearly indestructible, Land Rover. Eventually, and somehow, only five minutes late, she saw the signpost at the entrance to Manor Farm, and followed a long, pot-holed, gravel driveway that led to an unspectacular Georgian house, half-engulfed by ivy. She had barely got her camera bag out of the car and shut the door behind her when she heard excited barking and the scudding of many paws on gravel – a mixed pack of dogs surrounded her, an old black greyhound with a grey muzzle leading a couple of Labradors, a spaniel and a couple of rough-coated terriers.

'Don't mind the hounds; they'll only lick you to death.' Charlotte turned in the direction of the voice and saw a tall man in a flat cap strolling towards her. 'Down, Duke! Benson, no!' The dogs left her side – some ran back to their master while the greyhound set off in a fruitless pursuit of a rabbit that was safely out of range on the far side of the lawn. 'Hello Miss Bradley, I'm Gordon McKenzie.' He took off his cap to reveal a head of almost white hair.

'Pleased to meet you,' said Charlotte. 'Sorry I'm late,' She couldn't remember a man ever having doffed his cap to her before and she smiled – it seemed so old-fashioned, as did Mr. McKenzie's fashion sense - baggy plum cords with a tweed jacket and fawn loafers. From his grey hair and his weather-beaten features, she guessed he was well into his sixties.

'You found us, then? Marvellous,' he added without waiting for her to answer, even if her presence made the question somewhat redundant. 'So, a sundowner before we get started?'

'Probs not,' she said. 'The name says it all, doesn't it? If the sun's gone down I won't be able to take the photos.'

'Right. Follow me.' He cut through a gap in the thick hedge that surrounded the gardens, the dogs following on his heels, then set off at a brisk walk until they reached some paddocks. Three mares came ambling across the field to see them, their foals running around them, chasing each other like puppies. She looped her camera over her neck and began snapping away at them – the late evening sunshine was perfect, the mares' coats gleaming with an almost blue sheen.

'Shall we go in?' said Mr. McKenzie.

'No, this is fine,' said Charlotte, not wanting to admit that she felt far safer with the solid timber fencing between them. She'd been racing once with a bunch of friends, to Sandown Park one summer, where she'd been impressed by the speed and power of the horses, taking photos of them being washed down after their races, sweat dripping from their heaving sides, their nostrils flared and their eyes wild. These mares and foals looked much more amenable, away from the crowds and the adrenalin rush of the races, but centuries of selective breeding had made them unpredictable; a pigeon clattering out of the trees could instantly spook them and she'd be flattened.

'Well, shall I go in and stand them up for you?' asked Mr. McKenzie.

'Er... if you like,' she said. She wasn't sure what he meant – the horses were standing up, weren't they? – but she thought it might be something to do with the convention she'd seen in so many equestrian pictures, where the horse always faced from right to left and its legs were positioned so they were all visible from one side. It wasn't how she'd paint horses, given the chance; she preferred those sketch-like studies by Degas, fluid brushstrokes conveying that pent-up energy. Mr. McKenzie had said that what he really wanted was something in the style of Stubbs, who – in his opinion – was the greatest British artist. Charlotte had seen that Stubbs had painted a series of pictures of mares and foals in stylised classical landscapes; the horses were all in one plane, as if they had been placed on a stage set with a painted backdrop. She'd suggested this approach to Mr. McKenzie for his picture and he thought that it was a brilliant idea.

While she took more pictures, he squeezed his long body between the rails of the fence and the mares approached him. He caught one by its head-collar and pushed it back a couple of steps, so it was standing correctly. 'There you go, Miss Bradley,' he said. 'That's about right. This is Tuscan Sunset, with her colt foal by Nathaniel. She won four races and she's bred two winners from three foals. Her two-year-old runs at Haydock on Wednesday.'

Charlotte took a few quick snaps before the mare moved

out of position. She really knew nothing about racing and thought the mare's name sounded like a paint colour. She concentrated on taking photos and realised that, although she was more concerned with the effects of light and the balance of composition, Mr. McKenzie wanted photo-realistic, accurate portrayals of his individual animals 'Brief Interlude and filly by Masar,' said Mr. McKenzie, having let go of the first mare and manoeuvred another one into position. Charlotte knew it wouldn't be difficult to render the horses sufficiently accurately to be able to see which was which – the mares were different shades of brown, with varying amounts of white on their lower legs and white markings on their faces, but they were also different shapes and sizes; this second one was very tall and angular while the first one had been much more rounded and muscular. Charlotte zoomed in to get some headshots of the gangly mare and her foal. She noticed how alike they were; both had a similarly shaped white stripe that ran down the middle of their long faces and two white hindlegs, and the foal, on its disproportionately long legs, had clearly inherited its looks from its mother. But there was more. She zoomed in for some close-ups and could see that the mare and the foal had the same deep brown eyes; something that showed the connection in blood. It was even more noticeable when she looked away from the viewfinder and compared that foal with another one that had come over to investigate.

When the evening light had faded, they set off towards the house. Charlotte watched as the mares and foals walked slowly away. When she'd been to the races she'd never thought of those horses as playful foals who would eventually return to the pastures to breed their own foals, forgetting the training gallops and the cheering racecourse crowds, their names, which they never knew, living on in race results and pedigrees.

'All racehorses are descended from just three Arabian stallions imported in the Eighteenth Century,' said Mr. McKenzie as they neared the farmhouse. 'Nowadays every mating is witnessed and certified for the Stud Book and the foals are blood-typed and micro-chipped. Nothing can threaten the purity of the breed. Of course, we can only assume that the old breeders applied the same rigour. Now, time for that drink?'

'Thank you. Yes, just a quick one,' said Charlotte. The McKenzies were paying her several hundred pounds for a large painting, so it seemed rude to refuse their hospitality.

Mr. McKenzie led the way to the kitchen, where a slim woman in a green cardigan and a tweed skirt was opening a bottle of white wine.

'Ah, perfect timing, darling!' he said as he shut the door behind the last of the dogs. 'This is my wife, Penelope. Penny, this is Charlotte Bradley. She's taken loads of photos of the mares, ready for the painting.'

'Would you like a glass of wine?' said Mrs. McKenzie. 'It's a white Rioja. Quite pleasant. Gordon picked it up cheap at Waitrose.'

'Thank you,' said Charlotte, watching as she filled a huge glass for her. She tried to forget about the drive home on an empty stomach.

Mrs. McKenzie poured two more glasses and led the way to a large sitting room. 'Gordon thinks the picture will look good above the fireplace. It will be marvellous to finally get rid of that monstrosity,' she said, sneering at a Victorian hunting scene in a tarnished, overdone gilt frame. Charlotte thought that the portrayal of a huntsman in a red coat on a grey horse appeared lifeless, unlike the implied, impending movement in the Degas sketches that she loved, and without the anatomical accuracy of Stubbs. The horse's legs looked too thin, as if they would snap when it landed over the fence. She took a mouthful of the wine – it was crisp and sharp.

'Well, what do you think?' said Mrs. McKenzie.

'Hmm. Very nice. Quite citrusy,' said Charlotte.

'The painting, my dear, the painting. It is a truly hideous daub, isn't it?'

'Well... it's not really my taste. I suppose it's, er... of its time,' said Charlotte, hoping that sounded neutral enough.

'Huh – it wouldn't be so bad if it was valuable.'

'It's got sentimental value,' said Gordon. 'It's my great-great-grandfather, Colonel Vernon McKenzie, hunting the Mid Norfolk Foxhounds on his cavalry charger, Salamanca.'

'Salamander, I always call him,' said Mrs. McKenzie with a laugh that came out more as a loud snort.

'He lost half a leg at the Battle of Balaclava,' said Mr. McKenzie.

'The Colonel, not the horse,' added Penelope. 'And, Gordon, you know full well it was only his foot that got blown off. And now we know that old Vernon there can't be your ancestor, don't we?' She waved her hand at the painting as if she was shooing away a beggar. 'It's all very interesting, Miss Bradley,' she said.

'Oh, I'm sure our guest doesn't want to hear the family secrets,' said Gordon.

'Nonsense!' she replied, settling herself on the edge the sofa and beckoning to Charlotte to sit down next to her. 'Well, Gordon's great-grandfather, young Vernon, was an only child, born in 1859, three years after the end of the Crimean War. Old Vernon, the fellow in the painting there, came home, not only without a foot, but with a bad case of what they used to call shellshock. P.T.S.D. they'd call it now. And one symptom was that he'd completely lost his libido. Mind you, it didn't seem like he had many urges in the first place, before the war. Well, not normal, natural ones anyway.'

'Oh, this is all just old, old gossip,' said Gordon.

'It's all in those letters, dear. In black-and-white.' She turned to face Charlotte. 'We had a clear-out of the attic and found a box full of them, from old Vernon's wife to her older, married sister. God knows how and when they found their way back here, but they did. It's like some Victorian novel. Anyway, Clementine, the young naïve wife, writes to her sister about how the virile, dashing cavalry officer she's married can't, or won't, get his sabre out of its scabbard for her. So, she thinks it's her fault. She asks her sister for some tips on what to do in the bedroom. Despite some decidedly frank suggestions nothing seems to work. Then, one day, she goes to the stables to take her horse out for a hack, and she sees her husband going for it in the hay-barn with a groom. A young lad from the village. Can you imagine the scandal?

But the wise older sister tells her to say nothing if she values her comfortable lifestyle, so it's all kept quiet. Then Vernon goes off to the Crimea. Perhaps she hoped he'd get killed; who knows? There are no more letters until he returns – or most of him does – and they live out a charade of matrimonial bliss, as I suppose many couples did. Young Clementine stayed silent and got what she needed from other sources, with or without Vernon's knowledge. Then she fell pregnant.'

'So, who was the father?' asked Charlotte.

'Nobody knows. And we'll never know now,' said Penelope. 'Maybe the butler did it.' She downed what was left of her wine in one big gulp. 'Poor Clementine took her secret to her grave – she died of a fever when young Vernon was less than a year old, while old Vernon broke his neck in a hunting fall some years later.'

'What a happy story to tell our guest on such a pleasant spring evening,' said Gordon. 'How many women keep such secrets all their life? How many children grow up in total ignorance of their true parentage? What's that TV programme where they look into the ancestry of famous people?'

''Who do you think you are?'' suggested Charlotte.

'That's it,' said Gordon. 'Well, they always unearth some dark secrets, don't they? It makes good telly, I suppose. But it makes you think – there's a bloke in Australia who's the direct descendant of Richard III – he's a carpenter, I think. They checked his DNA after they dug the old king up out of that car park. So, some would say that this chap is the rightful King of England, and that ever since Bosworth it's been a trail of foreign interlopers – first the bloody Welsh and then the Germans – I don't know which are worse.' He stopped to look at the hunting painting. 'Ironic, isn't it? That painting of an unknowing imposter, who sired nobody, is going to be replaced by your picture of my Thoroughbreds, all of whom can trace their ancestry back at least three hundred years.'

'Miss Bradley, would you like another drink?' asked Mrs McKenzie.

'Thanks, but I must get going,' said Charlotte, getting to her feet and noticing how dark it was outside.

'Well, thank you so much for popping over,' said Mr. McKenzie as he led the way to the front door. He reached into his jacket pocket and handed her an envelope. 'A down payment,' he said.

'Oh, thank you...but that wasn't part of the arrangement.'

'I know, but I also know you'll have some costs. And you've got to eat.'

Charlotte got into her car and waved goodbye before she set off down the dark driveway, thinking that if Mr. McKenzie's great-great-granny hadn't pretended her child was her gay husband's then who knew what might have happened. The McKenzie's wouldn't be at Manor Farm, and they wouldn't be paying her to paint a picture of horses they didn't own which might not even exist. She picked up the envelope again. It felt surprisingly heavy.

Sylvia

Francis Thompson

Madeleine is my only child. Sadly, her marriage to Gerry didn't last. After they'd divorced, and against my advice, she kept in contact with her ex-husband. Gerry's second marriage came out of the blue. Madeleine was devastated. Sylvia, Gerry's new wife, wasn't a local girl. She just arrived on the scene one day. Dropped in from outer space, so to speak! There were rumours about Sylvia. Her being pregnant was the least toxic, and the gossipers' favourite. It proved to be false. The real reason for the marriage surfaced later. Sylvia had married Gerry, and not the other way around. She'd married him for his money. The woman was a bona fide gold digger. The marriage started badly when Gerry arrived thirty -three minutes late for their wedding. Sylvia was seething with anger and embarrassment, but despite of the evident acrimony between them, the ceremony went ahead. Better that it had been cancelled. Today, five years after his marriage to Sylvia, Gerry will arrive on time. He doesn't have a choice, it's his funeral.

It's early morning, almost 2am. I'm finding sleep elusive. Gerry's funeral is later in the day. The telephone on my bedside table is ringing. It'll be Madeleine bawling her eyes out over Gerry's death. I pick up the phone, I'm relieved to find that it's not Madeleine, but surprised to hear Gerry's sister Joan's voice.

'Ronnie,' she said. 'Apologies if I've woken you up. I'm phoning to warn you of a development.'

'A development?' I said half sleepily.

'Yes Ronnie. A development. This may come as a shock to you, but I've known for some time that Gerry and Sylvia's marriage was in fact bigamous. Legally your daughter, Madeleine, is now Gerry's widow. Sylvia doesn't know it yet, but Gerry's bank is in the process of freezing all her accounts. She's in big trouble. I hope she rots in hell. I'm emailing you the details. There's another matter of concern. In fact, it's a double-whammy. I'm certain that Gerry was murdered!' An interminable silence followed, then the line went dead. I tried phoning Joan back, but her line was either engaged, or the phone was off the hook. I suspected the latter.

The abrupt ending of my conversation with Joan felt pre-planned. I'd known her since childhood. She was shrewd, and had exited the conversation, just as I was about to ask her probing questions. Knowing I'd never get a wink of sleep during the rest of the night, I got out of bed, went downstairs to the kitchen, and brewed up a pot of strong coffee. There were no new emails.

My daughter's an accomplished photographer and wildly unpredictable. She isn't nicknamed, Mad-Eleine, without good reason. One of her foibles is obsessively collecting antique cameras. Her most recent acquisition is a sinister looking black Hasselblad. It resembles an exaggerated prop from a black and white Orson Welles' movie. It has a large, customised flash, which on occasions is known to hum ominously. I'm concerned Madeleine will turn up at the funeral with the Hasselblad dangling around her neck and wearing her bloodied Vivian Westwood top. The blood is real. Some of it belonged to Gerry.

I'd sunk my third coffee by the time Joan's email arrived.

As well as a covering note from Joan, she'd included extracts from two letters that apparently were winging their way to Sylvia. The first bore the imprimatur of 'The Divorce Court'.

<u>The Divorce Court.</u>

'For a marriage to be legally dissolved, it is necessary for the applicant' to file for their 'Decree Absolute' application, a minimum six weeks after their 'Decree Nisi' had been granted by The Court. The Court's attention has been brought to the fact that, in the above mentioned case, the aforementioned applicant had, either by design, or through a genuine mistake, filed for their 'Decree Absolute' application, only five weeks after the 'Decree' Nisi' had been granted. In-Law, this means that the original marriage is still intact, and any subsequent marriage is invalid.'

The second extract was to Sylvia from Gerry's Bank Manager.

All your <u>late partner's</u> accounts have been frozen pending the outcome of all the legal proceedings. This means that only an agreed monthly allowance can be granted you from your <u>late partner's</u> estate. This situation will continue until the legal position is resolved. I realise that this situation must be extremely distressing to you. This matter only came to our attention pursuant to a legal document served on us by solicitors, acting for <u>Madeleine Fisher Taylor</u>, who we are informed, is still the legal spouse of *your late partner.*

I printed out the email for future reference. The rational course of action was to phone Madeleine, but venturing down that cul-de-sac was a dead end. Communication with my daughter always goes to message service. An interesting morning lay ahead.

The Crestfallen Crematorium lay on the outskirts of town. The premises were formerly a small church. I've only viewed its crumbling facade from the outside. Some years ago there was a rumoured takeover by a Russian oligarch, it came to zilch, after he was found hanging upside down from Chelsea Bridge. Gerry's solicitor had given Joan carte blanche to organise his funeral. I found it surprising she'd chosen such an unattractive venue. It took me over thirty-five minutes to drive there. The cost of the mourner's fuel would probably eclipse the bill for Gerry's cremation.

My preference is to arrive early for important events or occasions. Gerry's service was listed for 11 am, so I arrived with forty minutes to spare. The poorly maintained driveway leading up to the Crematorium was littered with potholes, so I drove exceedingly slowly and carefully. There were around twenty empty vehicles in the car park. Signage was minimal. I parked so far away from the other cars that my green Volvo had quietly merged with the encroaching trees. I could see a group of about thirty of Gerry's family and friends gathered outside the entrance to the building. A few were smoking. The earlier service was obviously still ongoing. I wondered whether Sylvia and Joan were already inside the building and dealing with paperwork? After fifteen minutes of guilt inducing surveillance, I got out of the car and began walking across the tarmac, intending to join the assembled group. Mercifully so far, Madeleine was in absentia.

Crossing the car park, I heard a familiar female voice call my name. Turning around, I saw that it was Janice. The situation could be tricky. Janice is a very beautiful woman, a head-turner. I knew that Janice had been conducting a secret relationship with Gerry. They'd regularly booked into Room 7a at The Adelphi Hotel. I'd no idea if Sylvia knew of their affair. If she did, she kept schtum, probably because she was having it off with a hunky bartender in Room 11b at The Waverley Hotel. The reason I'm privy to this information is because of my darling daughter. It embarrasses me to admit it, but Madeleine secretly stalked both of these individuals. She stalked Gerry because she still loved him. She stalked Sylvia because she despised her. I've seen the clandestine photographs Madeleine has taken on her undercover excursions. Some are X rated. I think her ideal vocation would be working for either Scotland Yard or the CIA. I believe the Americans pay better.

Janice looked well, hair perfectly coiffured. I couldn't help admiring her expensive looking, full length, black leather coat. I wondered if she'd recently come into some money. When she caught up with me, we gave each other a hug. I failed to identify her perfume, but it smelt high-end. I ushered her aside, well away from the waiting group of mourners. I'd no idea how she'd react when I told her about Joan's phone call. I didn't want to frighten the horses, so I eased the topic into our conversation.

'Janice,' I said. 'It's hard to believe Gerry's gone. It's a tragedy. You do know who's to blame?'

'Who?'

'Sylvia.'

'Ronnie. Gerry had a heart attack. No one's to blame.'

'Heart attack my arse, Janice. I've been told Gerry was murdered.'

'Murdered?'

'Yes. Murdered. Don't speak so loudly.'

'No!'

'Yes. He was murdered.'

'Ronnie, why would someone murder Gerry?'

'Why do people usually get murdered?'

'How the hell would I know, Ronnie? I don't know anyone who's been murdered.'

'Money, Janice, money.'

'Jesus Christ, Ronnie. I only came along to pay my respects to Gerry. Now I'm up to my neck in talks about murder. You're not still on medication?'

'No. I'm bloody well not.'

'Well, it sounds like crackpot stuff, Ronnie. It's in really bad taste. Who'd do such a thing?'

'I've already told you. It was Sylvia.'

'How do you know this, Ronnie?'

'I got it from an impeccable source.'

'Who?'

'It was Gerry's sister, Joan. She phoned me in the early hours. We go way back. I went to school with her. Gerry was a toddler when their parents died. Joan was only twenty three years of age. She brought Gerry up as if he was her own child. Doted on him. Gave him security. I always admired Joan for that. She's a great woman.'

'And you believe her?'

'If Joan say's it's murder; I believe her.'

'What proof has she got? By the way, it's getting really cold. That earlier service is taking a long time to finish.'

'There could have been a murder, Janice. There's a lot of it about. Ha, ha, ha!'

'Jesus Ronnie! That's not funny. Are you certain you're not on medication?'

'Look over there, Janice. Sylvia's arriving, have you ever met her?'

'No, I haven't,' said Janice hesitatingly. 'I don't particularly want to either.'

'Notice anything, Janice?'

'Such as?'

'I'll give you a clue. Gerry was a fairly wealthy man.'

'And?' said Janice.

'Well, most grieving widows arriving for their husband's funeral would travel in a mode of transport more in keeping with their social status.'

'Oh, I see what you mean. She's arrived by taxi.'

'And, Janice, the driver's not getting a tip.'

'She's stingy?'

'Tight as a duck's arse, Janice. It looks like you've both got similar tastes.'

'I don't follow you, Ronnie?'

'Sylvia's wearing a full length, black leather coat. You look like her twin.'

'Oh God, Ronnie. She's coming in our direction.'

'Calm down. We might learn something.'

'Hello, Ronnie,' said Sylvia. 'It's a sad day. I see most of his close friends and family are here.'

'A good turnout, Sylvia. Gerry was a top man.'

'He was, Ronnie. He certainly was. You look cold.'

'Not the best of days, Sylvia; that's for sure. This is Janice, she was a friend of Gerry's.'

The two women greeted each other cordially. I noticed Sylvia's interest perk-up the moment that I'd mentioned Janice's name. She began nervously fidgeting with her wedding ring. Her eyes fixated on Janice's black leather coat.

'Hello Janice,' said Sylvia. 'I don't believe we've met.'

'We haven't.'

'I don't recall Gerry ever mentioning you,' said Sylvia.

'He wouldn't.'

'Why would that be?'

'I was his lover,' said Janice.

'One of many,' said Sylvia sarcastically, before turning on

her high-heels and storming off.

'Well, Janice,' I said. 'That's us both scrubbed from Sylvia's Christmas card list.'

'Thank God for that,' said Janice. 'By the way, there's some movement at the entrance. It looks like it's warm up time. If I stand here much longer, I'll need defrosting in a microwave.'

As we entered the building we were handed 'Order of Service' brochures. I gave mine a perfunctory glance, before slipping it into my jacket pocket. Thankfully being the last to enter, we'd managed to avoid being corralled into an uncomfortable seating arrangement. The church's old oak pews, divided by a central isle had been retained by the current owners. The front three pews on either side were occupied by Gerry's family and friends. Janice indicated where she'd prefer to sit. I followed her guidance. This meant that there were six empty pews between us and the others. I'd never been in a church-cum-crematorium before. Apart from the discoloured, but still beautiful, stained-glass windows, little remained of the building's original religious paraphernalia. Sadly, the alcoves within the church's walls, no longer contained their plaster saints or religious icons. I did notice however that the baptismal font, located to the right of the former altar, had been retained. I doubted it had tasted water for many years.

After we'd been sitting for some minutes, the music stopped abruptly. I'd the feeling something wasn't quite right. I was querying why no one had exited from the earlier service? Stranger still; Gerry's wicker coffin had already been set up on what looked like mechanical rollers. Next to it was a small table on which were photographs of Gerry.

The elevated lectern was to our front-left. I'd guessed correctly that Joan had already arrived. She was standing at the lectern, looking in our direction. I prayed she wasn't going to insist we vacate our seats and move further forward. I was relieved when she looked away.

Joan was a heavily built woman with an explosive temper. She wore black framed glasses with thick lenses which magnified her steely blue eyes. She was wearing a black, calf-length dress with a high neckline. Unlike Sylvia, who'd practically trademarked stilettos, Joan wore stylish flat shoes.

There were no hymn sheets on the pews. I was about to read my 'Order of Service' brochure, when Joan switched on the lectern's microphone and began speaking.

'On this sad occasion,' said Joan, speaking without notes, 'I'd like to say a few words in tribute to my younger brother, Gerry. Unfortunately, that's not possible. When all's said and done, my brother was a complete waster, and a compulsive liar. Dishonesty was second nature to Gerry. He regularly embezzled money from his many businesses; cheated on his first and only wife Madeleine, and his marriage to Sylvia was bigamous. I've no idea where Gerry acquired these qualities. It certainly didn't come from our parents, who were married in this very church. We did share one trait though, we both enjoyed a good joke, especially if it was in bad taste, and at the expense of others. The coffin in front of you is empty. Gerry was cremated at eight O'clock this morning. I arranged the earlier cremation to eliminate any possible forensic evidence. I've a confession to make to everyone. Gerry didn't die of a heart-attack, I murdered him. I won't go into any details. They could potentially incriminate me and be used as evidence in a trial. It's up to each one of you to decide whether this is a sick-joke, or the real thing. On a lighter note, everyone, including Sylvia, is invited to the funeral reception afterwards at The Waverley Hotel. Gerry's widow, Madeleine, will be taking the photographs.'

In the Wash

Emma Veit

- First prize -

'Alright, who is she?'

They're sitting side by side in the launderette watching socks, undies and t-shirts tossed repeatedly and soullessly in the air of the dryer. They used to do this together years ago, sent here by mum with a handful of change and a stream of threats against spending it on sweets, cigarettes or porn. The concrete floor and the damp air smells the same as it did then: alkaline, bleach, despair.

'She's no one to you, Alice. Leave it be, eh?'

He's wearing his old uniform from his teenage years of tracksuit bottoms, grimy trainers and a sweatshirt from the gym he used to hang out at. She knows he hasn't been there recently because Graham would've told her. There's no love lost between her brother and her man.

'What've you got in the dryer? Doesn't she do yer washing for yer?'

'No. Why would she?' He shifts nervously from one bum cheek to another. She always knew when he was lying when they were kids; knows it now, too.

She tuts, stares at the demented washing, spinning and falling. Waits him out. He holds out longer than she expects.

'How's the kids then?' he asks, shifting again, scuffing the toe of his shoe on the unforgiving floor, his foot at an awkward angle.

She doesn't say, 'What do you care?' though she wants

to. She takes a deep breath in, swallowing the scent of his body spray and sweat along with the laundry detergent swirling in the air around them. 'Sophie's started ballet. She loves it, but she's like a heffalump on steroids, prancing about in her tutu and leotard. Ben's in school, did you know?'

'S'pose he is and all. Does he like it?'

'He gets on alright. He's bringing a reading book home already. Won't sit down and read it, but he brings it home and looks at the pictures at breakfast. How many kids does she have?'

He takes a breath in to answer; closes his mouth; opens it again. She thinks he looks like a cartoon fish, caught on a hook.

'Why do you care about some woman you saw me with, one time? It's not a big deal, Alice.' She wants so badly to pinch him, her fingers twitch.

'Not a big deal, is it?' It's always so bloody hot in these goddamn places, walls of machines using up energy, pumping out hot air and steam and too much fucking noise.

'You're married to the poor sap, and it's no big deal? You call me once a month, all these years, natter on about some bullshit mates, your stupid job, your sorry lack of love life, and all along, you're married with how many fucking children?'

'Alright, Jesus, calm the fuck down.' He looks over his shoulder, both ways - there's no one else in the building, for fucksake.

'Don't tell me to calm down or I'll sock you one. When

did you marry her?'

'We're not, like, proper married. I mean, we are, but we aren't. It's complicated.'

'Yeah, right. Complicated.' She rolls her eyes so hard her eyeballs hurt. 'I just don't understand you. A secret wife? And kids? It's just so much utter bollocks, Jol. Why would you keep them a secret from me? Me? What did I ever do to make you keep a whole family secret from me?'

He's pushing the rubber of his trainer so hard into the floor she thinks he'll bruise his toe, the idiot. Face like a smacked arse. She's getting to him.

'It's my job, alright? It's a secret because it's part of the job. I'm deep in, and I can't risk anyone knowing. Specially you.' He glowers at her, leaps up and heads out the door, lighting a fag and leaving it dangling between his soft lips as he paces up and down, staring at his phone screen.

She's startled into immobility. Just watches the lad through the dirty window, pacing up and down, passers-by exaggeratedly stepping away from him.

She pulls out her own phone and opens Facebook to the image she'd found. The woman looks happily up at the photographer, her smile split by the crack in her phone screen, her blonde hair faded in the captured sunlight. There's a kid in a pushchair in front of her, sticky faced and fingered. It looks like they're at the fair. She's wearing some kind of knitted or crocheted pullover, the sort of thing a hippie would wear in her mum's youth. She wonders who took the photo. Was it Jol? He's never on Facebook though. Would rather put needles in his eyes.

The lad comes back in and slumps down in the plastic

chair beside her. She's switched her phone off and put it away before he can ask anything.

'What did she do?'

He looks at her, surprise in his watery eyes and flared nostrils. 'Who?'

'The woman. The wife. What did she do?' She gets annoyed that he doesn't understand her, and it puts a knife in her tone. 'Why are the police investigating her? What awful thing has she done that they've sent you in...' She scoffs at his expression. She can't tell which part he's outraged by, but she knows he wants to hit her. Wouldn't be the first time.

'She ain't done nothing, Alice! Leave off, for Christ's sake. It's not her, it's who she knows, alright? You can't stick your fat nose in this, it's nothing to do with you. I mean it. Leave it alone.'

His dryer beeps its discordant end song and he leaps up and grabs hold of a broken plastic basket. He wrenches the door open and grabs his clothes, stuffing them into the basket with angry, jerky movements. She stands too, leans against the high counter and helps him fold his washing. T-shirts; undies; a pair of jeans, faded and soft with wear. None of it is his uniform, which he used to be so proud of.

'Al, listen. It's serious, alright? What I'm doing with her. It's dangerous. I'm walking a line. I need to keep them safe, and me, and I need to do my job. I can't let anything get in the way. When it's done, when there's some bodies in the clink, then I'll get it sorted. Maybe I can introduce you then. But until it's done, you have to trust me. Leave it alone. Yeah?'

She's quiet for a bit. Trying to make her thoughts form into words. The warm cotton falls into shape in her hands automatically as she reaches, folds, smooths, piles. This is my little brother, she keeps telling herself. She's wiped his nose and eyes, cleaned up his scrapes and scratches. Stole condoms for him. Cleaned up his sick. She's loved him all her life without ever considering why.

Does she love him? Should she?

'Jol,' she says, his name soft on her tongue. 'Does she know who you are? Does she know what you're doing?'

The fury of the guilt reddens his face again.

'Of course, she fucking doesn't! Do you think she would've let me get anywhere near her if she knew I was a fucking copper? You don't get the job at all do you? You never have. Jesus Fucking Christ!'

They're quiet again. An old lady tries to get through the door, back half bent over a large shopper. Her brother opens it for her and cold air from outside swirls into the steam. By the time he gets back to his clothes she's finished the job. They're all neatly folded and packed away into his rucksack.

'Thanks,' he says.

'S'alright.'

He checks his phone, shuffles his feet. 'I'd best crack on then.'

'Yeah, me too.'

A sudden gust of wind hammers the rain against the window, filling the grey silence between them.

'Thanks,' he says again. He bends down to kiss her on the cheek, his bristles scraping briefly against her soft skin. He smells like tobacco and rain. 'I'll call you, yeah?'

'Yeah,' she says. 'Bye.'

He's gone out the door and heading up the street, the opposite way she expected him to go, head bent against the storm blowing straight at him.

She sits down again, feeling no rush to leave the unexpected nostalgia of the launderette. Graham's taken the kids to his mum's for the day. She was meant to go shopping. A new dress for his 50th. Her heart's not in it now.

She pulls out her phone again, opens it to the image of the happy, hippy-looking woman. Stares at the sticky-faced child. Clicks through to the Facebook page she found it on.

Before she can think too hard, she's done a friend request.

If it was her, she thinks, if she was that woman, she would want to know. She's clicked on to Messenger before she's aware of deciding to. She's opened a can of worms now; may as well eat them.

Does she love her brother?

She really isn't sure.

She wonders if the woman in the picture loves him either.

The Lion's Share

Angela Wray

'What do you mean, you can't have her for Easter – it's all arranged! You promised, Charles, you bastard...'

Divina, carefully dusting the base of the Lalique table lamp, tried to appear invisible as her employer strode about the blue drawing room, phone in one hand, cigarette in the other. This was not the first argument Divina had heard between Lady Lincoln and her ex-husband, father of her only child, Isabella. Divina wondered if Lady Lincoln was actually aware that she was in the same room, as her employer's voice rose to screaming pitch.

'No, fuck you, I can't have her here! I've got the Underwoods coming, and you know they can't stand children. I'm off to Mustique the day after they leave, and I can't possibly take her with me...'

There was a loud rumble on the other end of the phone and Divina tensed as she clutched her duster, waiting for the blast of invective that was the next phase in the conversation.

'You fucking cunt, it's my money and I can do what I like with it! If you're so keen for her to come to Mustique with me, you can pay for her and for the hire of a nanny while we're there. No, I didn't think you would, you tight bastard. I suppose you've spent all this month's allowance on the gee-gees and that little bitch you sniff around. Well bad luck, you're having your daughter for Easter whether you like it or not...'

Lady Lincoln ended the call and ground the cigarette

butt into the Murano glass ashtray. Divina caught her eye unwittingly.

'Tidy this away, please, Divina,' her employer said briskly, 'and don't forget to change the sheets in the Moroccan bedroom; the Underwoods are coming tomorrow. And make sure the kitchen is pristine for when the caterers arrive in the morning. Oh, and Isabella comes home from school today. You'd better give her clean sheets, although as she's going to her father's tomorrow, it hardly seems worth it. Also, I think it's time we cleared out the back attic. All Isabella's baby toys are up there; just send them to the charity shop, will you. Children First is the one I'm patron of, so you'd better call them - someone will come and collect if you mention my name. Now, please be very quiet and don't clump about with the vacuum; I'm shattered, and I need to rest before the opera tonight. You are available to babysit, aren't you?'

Without waiting for an answer or even a nod from Divina, Lady Lincoln left the room. There was a barked final order from the hallway, 'Oh, and don't forget to polish the cutlery for tomorrow – we'll need it all as there are eighteen for dinner.'

'Yes, Madam.' Divina shook her head and smiled to herself. She was glad that she was not Lady Lincoln with her social maelstrom of a life and her complicated family arrangements, and her enormous houses, and her live-in servants. Far from feeling resentful or used, as she worked Divina reflected on how lucky she was. Lady Lincoln was in many ways a good employer: she provided Divina with her own room, and paid her enough to live on and to send a proportion back to her family in Manila. Divina was allowed use of the computer in Lady Lincoln's study to

Skype them once a week. Her dream was to save enough for her husband and two children to come over to the UK and for him to find a job in London so that – joy of joys! – they could all be reunited. Divina prayed nightly and fervently that God would allow this to happen. So far, He had not answered, but Divina's faith was unshakeable; she knew it was just a matter of time.

Late that afternoon she climbed the staircase that led to the back attic and opened the door. This part of the house was new to her – in the five years she had worked for Lady Lincoln there had been no need to come up here. She switched on the light and gasped at the bounty that lay before her: paintings in gold frames propped against the walls, rows of ornately carved chairs, tea chests full of china and glass. And the toys! Teddy bears by the dozen stuffed into boxes, magnificently dressed dolls with the most complicated hairstyles, a coach-built dolls' pram, a tricycle, and an exquisite dolls' tea service in a box that looked as if had never been touched. Goodness, how her children would love this treasure trove! Divina dutifully started to carry the toys down to the back hall, ready for the Children First van to collect them the next morning.

She'd almost finished and was scanning the attic for anything she might have missed, when she saw a golden, tufted tail poking out from behind one of the pictures. She eased back the picture – it was a drawing signed 'Picasso', a strange, scribbly thing she thought – and there lay a beautiful, majestic lion pyjama case. One of his eyes was coming loose, giving him a lop-sided look, but he had the most gorgeous golden mane and Divina stroked it lovingly. She picked the lion up. He was heavier than she expected, and his stomach certainly didn't contain one of

Isabella's long forgotten nighties. It felt lumpy and hard.

'Diveeeena!' came a joyful shout from downstairs.

'Up here!' Divina shouted back, dusting herself off as she stood up. Isabella appeared in the doorway, her plaits dishevelled, green school blazer a little tighter than Divina remembered from the beginning of term.

'Divina!' Isabella rushed forward and threw her arms round her. Divina laughed and kissed the top of her head.

'Now, let me look at you, Miss Isabella. I think you are turning into quite a young lady. And look how your hair has grown!'

'Well, look - I can nearly sit on it!' said Isabella, tugging the band from each of her plaits, then shaking the hair out into a haze of golden curls. She smoothed it down her back and Divina grinned, holding up the pyjama case. 'It's just like the lion's fur,' she said.

Isabella took the lion and looked at it. 'I've never seen this – is it yours?'

'No,' laughed Divina. 'I'm not a little girl anymore.'

'Nor am I, I'm eight, but I still have a pijjy case, and it's much nicer than this old thing. Look how lumpy his tummy is, and it's all sewn up – you couldn't get your nightie in it, even if you wanted to.'

'Darling, where are you?' came Lady Lincoln's voice from the landing below.

'Hello, Mummy! I'm up in the attic with Divina.' She ran down the stairs and hugged her mother.

'Oh darling, please, not so tight; this dress creases

dreadfully.' Lady Lincoln looked magnificent in a long, cerise silk shift. She kissed her daughter on the cheek, then stood back, holding her round the shoulders as she looked her up and down. Isabella grinned and bounced on her toes, the pyjama case dangling from her hand. Divina smiled wistfully, wondering what her own eight-year-old daughter was doing at this moment.

'Goodness, your hair's grown, darling. Divina, please make an appointment for Isabella to visit the hairdresser the day before she goes back to school.'

'Yes, Madam.'

'But Mummy, I like it this long. I can nearly...'

'No buts, darling.' She caught sight of the lion dangling from the child's hand. 'God, that old thing! It used to live in the nursery when I was a child. Didn't like it much, too lumpy. It belonged to Granny Estelle. I think there's a picture of her in the green drawing room with her parents. That was one of the great family scandals, but you'll have to wait until you're older before I tell you about it. Now, darling, be good for Divina tonight - I have to go to a very tedious party and then the opera, so I shan't be home until late.'

'Oh but Mummy, why can't I hear the scandal about Granny Estelle and the lion?'

Lady Lincoln laughed.

'You are a funny little thing – the scandal is about something quite different. Divina, just throw it out with the rest of the toys please. Unless you want to keep it,' she added.

'Oh, Lady Lincoln, how kind! I could send him to my

children, they would love to play with him.'

'Are you sure? Wouldn't they prefer something in better condition? It's a moth-eaten old thing, looks rather sad, doesn't it, darling?'

Isabella nodded, grimacing. 'I don't like him much. His mane's scary.' She handed it back to Divina.

Divina took the lion up to her room. He did look sad and moth-eaten, but his face was kind and she was certain that her children would love him. She held him at arm's length.

'I shall call you Leo,' she said. 'Now Leo, you are too heavy to send to the Philippines, so tonight I am going to perform an operation on you. It's all right – you won't feel a thing – but you will be much comfier on your journey.'

Later on, when Isabella had finally stopped chattering and was asleep in her room, Divina picked open Leo's stomach with nail scissors, giggling as she imagined that she was a surgeon performing a tricky procedure. From the patient's stomach Divina extracted a brown paper bag. She opened it. Inside, there was a package rolled in sheets of newspaper, which she unrolled carefully. Individually wrapped like boiled sweets in several layers of tissue paper were Leo's lumps, about twenty of them. She unwrapped one and gasped. An emerald! No, surely just something from a child's broken necklace. She unwrapped another, then another, until the whole of Leo's stomach contents was exposed on the bedspread: rubies, sapphires, even the odd diamond. Divina smiled. She would have them restrung, and one day, the day that her daughter arrived in London, she would give her the necklace and tell her where it came from. She dropped the stones back in the bag and put it on her bedside table, next to her Bible.

The following day Divina was dusting the green drawing room ready for the guests' arrival when she remembered Granny Estelle. The painting over the fireplace was of an extremely handsome man with a magnificent moustache, holding a rifle and looking very pleased with himself. At his feet lay a dead tiger. A beautiful woman was gazing at him adoringly. In the background was a whole army of servants, one of whom had a little girl by the hand, a little girl with beautiful long, golden curls. 'Estelle,' whispered Divina, wondering if the child was as unloved as Isabella. The painting was entitled The Maharajah of Kashgar and the Duchess of Aberfeldy.

On her next day off, Divina took the stones to be restrung. The jeweller looked at her suspiciously.

'Where did you get these?' he asked.

Divina always thought it best to tell the truth, for that was the way you got to Heaven.

'My employer, Lady Lincoln. They were found in a pyjama case in the attic.'

The jeweller laughed. 'Well, they really are exquisite,' He held the stones in his hand and peering at them through his eyeglass. 'I've never seen jewels of such high quality in this country.'

Divina's heart gave a massive lurch, and everything went black. She shut her eyes and told herself to stay calm. She decided to be open and honest with the jeweller.

'They came from India, from the Maharajah of Kashgar,' said Divina.

'Really? Now that is interesting. I remember the name – I think there may have been some sort of scandal in the past – an affair or some such, and a child born out of wedlock. Mixed race - long ago and far away, eh - happens all the time now.' He looked at Divina with a raised eyebrow. Divina hadn't a clue what he was talking about, but smiled, hoping that was the right thing to do. 'Anyway,' he continued, more briskly, 'I'll have them ready for you next Friday, if that's convenient.'

'Thank you,' smiled Divina.

How could she wait a whole week without telling anyone? She thought she might burst. There was plenty to do, however, as Lady Lincoln had left her a long list of spring-cleaning jobs that had to be completed before she came back from Mustique. Divina worked diligently, and on the Friday she collected the necklace and took it to a dealer in Hatton Garden to be valued. Again, she was honest, telling the dealer that it was a gift from Lady Lincoln and that it came from India, from the Maharajah of Kashgar, and she showed the dealer the newspaper the stones had been wrapped in, The Times of India dated 10th September 1895. The dealer looked at Divina and smiled at her honest face, and said he had a client who might well be interested in purchasing it, and that he would be able to offer twenty thousand pounds as it really was a very special piece.

Divina took a deep breath and tried to hold her voice steady as she told the dealer she would think about it. On the bus home, guilt began to creep over her like a rash, which became itchier the more she thought about it. On Saturday she went to confession.

'Father,' she murmured, 'I was given a gift, and it is worth much more money than I thought. I am worried that I might be committing a sin unless I return it to the person who gave it to me.'

'Oh no, my child,' came the immediate answer. 'If it was a gift given with genuine good intention, the value of it is immaterial. Whatever its worth, you are entitled to keep it. Money is not a valued commodity in the Bible, as you know, nor are those who accumulate wealth. I'm sure you're familiar with the passage from St Mark's gospel, when our Lord says that it is easier for a camel to pass through the eye of a needle than for a rich man to enter the kingdom of God. Perhaps the person who gave you the gift realizes its worth and is trying to follow the teaching of Jesus that to enter the kingdom of Heaven, you must give away your earthly treasures. Now, enjoy the gift and perhaps you could give a little more than usual in the collection plate this Sunday to assuage any residual guilt.'

'Thank you, Father, I'll certainly do that.' Divina didn't understand the last few words but got the message from the one word that she did understand – guilt. She assuaged it at holy communion the next morning with a £20 note which she placed in the collection plate, trying to appear nonchalant whilst inwardly jubilant with the thrill of profligacy.

Other titles from the Cambridge Writers Group

(Available from Amazon)

COINCIDENCE: Cambridge Writers Short Story Competition 2022
VISITORS: Cambridge Writers Short Story Competition 2021
MOUNTAIN: Cambridge Writers Short Story Competition 2020
REVENGE: Cambridge Writers Short Story Competition 2019
FREEDOM: Cambridge Writers Short Story Competition 2018
Compilation of Cambridge Writers Short Story Competition Winners 2013-2017

Printed in Great Britain
by Amazon

33562818R00099